Thomas the Tank Engine
CROSS STITCH

Thomas the Tank Engine
CROSS STITCH

20 exclusive designs based on the Railway Series by the Rev. W. Awdry

Helena Turvey

HAMLYN

I dedicate this book to my son Alex, who has had a hard journey to travel during the making of this book and a special thanks to the children and staff at Treliske hospital, Truro, for helping him on his road to recovery.

THOMAS THE TANK ENGINE CROSS STITCH
Helena Turvey

First published in Great Britain in 1995 by Hamlyn
an imprint of Reed Consumer Books Limited
Michelin House, 81 Fulham Road, London SW3 6RB
and Auckland, Melbourne, Singapore and Toronto

Art Editor LISA TAI
Editor SOPHIE PEARSE
Executive Editor JUDITH MORE
Executive Art Editor LARRAINE SHAMWANA
Photography DEBI TRELOAR
Styling FRANCESCA MILLS
Illustration PAM WILLIAMS
Production CANDIDA LANE

A CIP record for this book is available from the British Library

ISBN 0 600 58856 4
ISBN 0 600 58891 2 (Paperback)

The publishers have made every effort to ensure that all instructions given in this book are accurate and safe, but they cannot accept liability for any resulting injury, damage or loss to either person or property whether direct or consequential and howsoever arising. The author and publishers will be grateful for any information which will assist them in keeping future editions up to date.

Typeset in Bauer Bodoni and Gill Sans
Printed and bound in Spain by Cayfosa

Contents

Foreword

About of measles was the starting point of what are, without doubt, among the most successful and best-loved children's stories of our times. The Reverend Awdry first invented a story about an engine called Edward to take his son's mind off the misery of having measles. The impromptu bedside story then led to the making of a wooden push-along model of Edward, and then another of a tank engine named Thomas. Fifty years later, the fertile imaginations of father and son have left a legacy of dozens of stories which have sold in their millions. Much more than this however, long after the demise of the steam train and the closure of branch lines in Britain, the exploits of the engines in the

Railway Series are a cherished part of the great wide world of children's fiction today, as well as a continuing source of delight and nostalgia for adults.

This book echoes some of most popular scenes from the engine stories, and here, some of the favourite characters and episodes from the Railway Series are presented in twenty exciting cross stitch designs. There are pictures to frame and hang, items of practical clothing that children will enjoy wearing, a range of delightful gifts to make and beautiful soft furnishings to sew.

The projects will appeal both to beginners and the more experienced cross stitcher. If you are a novice, then it is a good idea to start with one of the smaller and simpler projects, which include the happy birthday card and the snowdrift Christmas card, the whistle key ring, the Gordon cake band and the Fat Controller book mark.

A beginner's project will be quick to make and involves minimal sewing in order to make up. In addition, there are three quite simple designs you can make which require no sewing beyond the cross stitching – all you have to do is mount and frame them to enjoy as pictures. Success with the easier projects will encourage you to attempt the intermediate projects such as the Thomas and Clarabel scarf, the drawstring purse which is decorated with Harold the helicopter, the green flag

lampshade or the James T-shirt. With some sewing ability you can tackle a more advanced project like the vivid green baseball cap which shows Henry stuck in a tunnel, the Henry and the elephant cushion, the stop and go slippers, or the Thomas pencil case which any child would be proud to take to school. All the finished items have been photographed in a glorious blaze of primary colours which will appeal to children and I hope will entice cross stitch enthusiasts to start stitching. The designs also complement each other by theme and colour scheme so, for instance in the Soft Furnishings chapter, the cushion will offset the lampshade, the curtains or the toy bag in a child's room or a playroom. And the clothes featured in the Clothing chapter can be worn in combination – why not combine the bright red scarf and the baseball cap, the T-shirt and the dungarees or the pyjamas and felt slippers? Some projects are even suitable for children to cross stitch themselves, provided, of course, that they have adult supervision and help in making up the finished items. A child at heart, I have relished re-reading our *Thomas the Tank Engine* collection and I greatly enjoyed the challenge of creating the projects in this

book inspired by the stories. I hope that both you and your children together will enjoy reading the book and get pleasure and ideas of your own from making some of the designs.

Helena Turvey

Pictures

Opposite An attractive pair of pictures, on the left is Stepney the "Bluebell" engine and on the right Gordon, Henry and James after a night's sleep in the yard. Feel free to adapt any of the other projects that appear in the book into pictures – once you have completed the cross stitch, all you need to do is mount and frame them.
Below An original illustration from the story *Bowled Out* which was the inspiration for the Stepney cross stitch picture shown opposite.

Many of the projects in this book involve a sewing-together stage after you have finished the actual embroidery. However, if you prefer just to cross stitch, working all sorts of beautiful coloured threads on canvas into a variety of *Thomas the Tank Engine* scenes, then why not attempt to make one or even both of the pictures in this chapter? The first shows Stepney the "Bluebell" engine who pays a visit from the Bluebell Railway, where old engines are conserved. The second picture shows a trio of favourite engines – Gordon, Henry and James. Gordon is awake, Henry is beside him still asleep and James is yawning widely. Just follow the colour charts and the thread keys to complete the pictures and then mount and frame them. You can use cross stitch pictures to decorate a shelf, a mantlepiece or any other surface alongside other *Thomas the Tank Engine* items, if you collect them. For a third picture design turn to pages 50-51 which is an adaptation of the pencil case project. To preserve your work and keep it clean and pressed you should frame pictures behind glass as this protects them from getting grubby or dusty.

Stepney Picture

This picture is from the story *Bowled Out*. "The big Diesel surveyed the shed. 'Not bad,' he said. 'I've seen worse. At least you are all clean.' The engines gaped. 'It's not your fault,' he went on, 'but you're all out of date. Your Controller should scrap you, and get engines like me...' Diesel saw his coaches waiting at the platform. He rolled proudly towards them. 'Look at me, Duck and Stepney,' he purred. 'Now I'll show you something.' He advanced a few yards, then suddenly he coughed – faltered – choked – and stopped. The Inspector meanwhile had seen nothing of this. He was looking for his hat. 'Can we help you at all?' asked Duck and Stepney sweetly. Diesel seethed with baffled fury as they pushed him back to the shed. 'My hat!' exclaimed the Inspector, as the cavalcade went by. 'Bother your hat!' said the Fat Controller crossly. 'The train's due out in ten minutes, and you'll have to take it, Duck.' Duck looked doubtful, but when Stepney asked, 'Can I help him, Sir?' he felt better. The Fat Controller was pleased too, and hurried away almost cheerfully to make the arrangements "

From *Stepney the "Bluebell" Engine* by The Rev. W. Awdry

A scene of Stepney the "Bluebell" engine which is set off with a bright red mount and hung above railway trinkets.

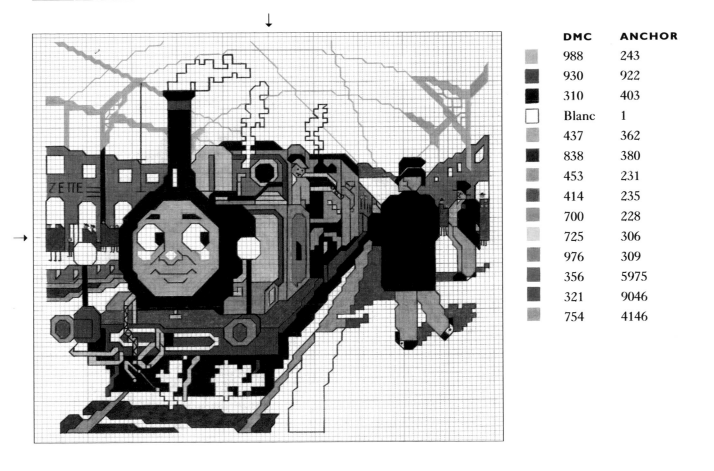

DMC	ANCHOR
988	243
930	922
310	403
Blanc	1
437	362
838	380
453	231
414	235
700	228
725	306
976	309
356	5975
321	9046
754	4146

ABILITY LEVEL: *Easy*

MEASUREMENTS

The cross stitch design measures 14 x 15cm
(5⅝ x 6 in)

MATERIALS

• Basic sewing kit (see page 92)
• One piece of 16-count Aida, 41 x 28cm
  (16⅜ x 11¼in), in cream
• Stranded cotton, one skein of each of the
  colours shown in the key (above right)
• Tapestry needle, size 24-26
• A 15cm (6in) embroidery hoop

TO EMBROIDER

Follow the chart and the key (which gives the colour codes for the cotton threads). Separate out two strands of thread from a single skein for the cross stitch, see page 95. Work the green arches using two strands in backstitch, see page 95. Outline in backstitch using a single strand of black. Outline the smoke and the top hat using a single strand, working in light gray. For the people's faces, and the yellow on the front and side of the train, make French knots using two strands of thread and twisting the thread twice around the needle, see page 97.

TO MAKE UP

1. Bind the raw edges of the Aida, as explained on page 90.

2. Centre the design on the piece of Aida, see page 93.

3. Fix the hoop around the middle of the area to be stitched and start to cross stitch in the centre of the piece of Aida.

4. Treat the finished embroidery as described on page 94.

5. Stretch the canvas, then mount and frame the picture as required.

11

Wake Up James Picture

This picture shows sleepy James yawning in his shed, alongside Gordon and Henry; it is taken from the story *James and the Express*. "Sometimes Gordon and Henry slept in James's shed, and they would talk of nothing but boot-laces! James would talk about engines who got shut up in tunnels and stuck on hills, but they wouldn't listen, and went on talking and laughing. 'You talk too much, little James,' Gordon would say. 'A fine strong engine like me has something to talk about. I'm the only engine who can pull the express. When I'm not there, they need two engines. Think of that! I've pulled expresses for years and have never once lost my way. I seem to know the right line by instinct,' said Gordon proudly. Every wise engine knows, of course, that the signalman works the points to make engines run on the right lines, but Gordon was so proud that he had forgotten. 'Wake up, James,' he said next morning, 'it's nearly time for the express. What are you doing? Odd jobs? Ah well! We all have to begin somewhere, don't we! Run along now and get my coaches...' James went to get Gordon's coaches. They were now all shining with lovely new paint."

From *James the Red Engine* by The Rev. W. Awdry

Taken from the story James and the Express, here is a trio of favourite engines – Gordon, Henry and yawning James, waking up in the yard.

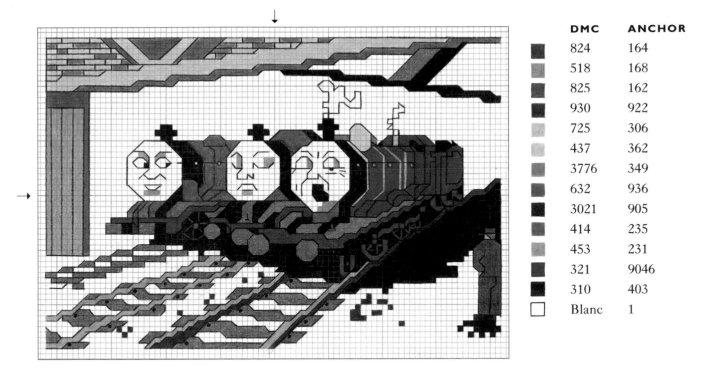

DMC	ANCHOR
824	164
518	168
825	162
930	922
725	306
437	362
3776	349
632	936
3021	905
414	235
453	231
321	9046
310	403
Blanc	1

ABILITY LEVEL: *Easy*

MEASUREMENTS

The cross stitch design measures 12.8 x 8.3cm (3¼ x 5in)

MATERIALS

• Basic sewing kit (see page 92)
• One piece of 16-count Aida, 39 x 23cm (15⅝ x 9¼in), in gray
• Stranded cotton, one skein of each of the colours shown in the key (above right)
• Tapestry needle, size 24-26
• A 15cm (6in) embroidery hoop

TO EMBROIDER

Outline the smoke and the bricks in a single strand of white, work in backstitch, see page 95. Work the wheel spokes using two strands in backstitch. The red lines on the blue trains and the yellow lines on the red train are worked in two strands in backstitch. Work the black on the trains' faces in two strands in backstitch. Use a single strand to work the rails in backstitch, and two strands of light gray in backstitch for the rails. For the closed eyes, the side rails on the train engines and the bolts on the sleepers, make French knots with two strands, twisting the yarn twice around the needle, see page 97. For the side rails on James's engine work French knots in two strands with two twists around the needle.

TO MAKE UP

1. The size given for the Aida leaves room for fixing the hoop and framing. First centre the design on the Aida; measure carefully and use basting lines as a positional guide, see page 93.

2. Fix the hoop centrally around the area to be stitched and begin.

3. Treat the finished embroidery as described on page 94.

4. Stretch the finished canvas before you mount and frame the picture as you desire. Note that if you cross stitch the picture on a piece of 14-count Aida then the finished design will be slightly larger, and will measure approximately 16.5 x 11.5cm (6⅝ x 4⅝in).

Clothing

Above This illustration showing James being bothered by a swarm of bees comes from the story *Buzz Buzz* and relates to the James T-shirt project overleaf.
Opposite A variety of the projects that feature in this chapter; there are all sorts of colourful and practical clothes to embroider and make yourself that children will love to wear.

All the projects featured in this chapter rely on the use of waste canvas, see page 90. This useful material allows you to embroider directly onto a wide range of fabrics. Once you have mastered how to use waste canvas you can begin to embellish all sorts of items of clothing, whether you buy them off the peg or make them up yourself from a pattern.

The following pages provide original ideas for decorating the sorts of clothing that children enjoy wearing. The T-shirt, pyjamas, scarf and dungarees require no sewing to complete – you simply embroider the cross stitch designs directly onto the purchased pieces of clothing. The bib involves some simple sewing, and to complete the more advanced projects such as the baseball cap and the slippers just follow the step-by-step sewing techniques. After some practice you can start to add scenes from favourite *Thomas the Tank Engine* stories to other types of clothing. Using this chapter as inspiration, you can give pockets, shorts, shirts, hats, gloves, jackets and more an individual touch with a railway scene of your choice.

James T-shirt

Of the many James stories, one of the most memorable is *Buzz Buzz*. "...Two porters were taking a loaded trolley to the front van... 'Careful, Fred! Careful!' warned Bert, but Fred was in a hurry and didn't listen. Suddenly an old lady appeared in front. Fred stopped dead, but the luggage slid forward and burst the lid of a large white wooden box. Some bees flew out, and just as James came backing down, they began to explore the station... They found the empty station cold. James's fireman was trying to couple the train. They buzzed round him hopefully. They wanted him to mend their hive. Then they could go back and be warm

again... The bees, disappointed, turned their attention to James. James's boiler was nice and warm. The bees swarmed round it happily. 'Buzz off! BUZZ OFF!' he hissed... At last one settled on his hot smokebox. It burnt its feet. The bee thought James had stung it on purpose. It stung James back – right on the nose! 'Eeeeeeeeeeeeeee!' whistled James."

From *Main Line Engines* by The Rev. W. Awdry

James is a beautiful bright red engine and looks very smart cross-stitched onto a plain white T-shirt.

DMC	ANCHOR
321	9046
725	306
415	398
414	235
437	362
310	403
Blanc	1

ABILITY LEVEL: *Easy*

MEASUREMENTS

The cross stitch design measures 12.5 x
6cm (5 x 2⅜in)

MATERIALS

- Basic sewing kit (see page 92)
- One piece of 14-count waste canvas,
  20 x 10cm (8 x 4in), in white
- One piece of interfacing 20 x 10cm (8 x 4in)
- An embroidery hoop to fit the T-shirt
- Stranded cotton, one skein of each of the
  colours shown in the key (above right)
- Tapestry needle, size 24-26
- One white jersey T-shirt (toddler's size)

TO EMBROIDER

Use two strands of thread for the main
embroidery worked in cross stitch, see
page 95. The cloud is worked using a
single strand of dark gray in backstitch,
see page 95. The face is backstitched in
two strands of black and the rest of the
black embroidery is worked with one
strand of black in backstitch. To highlight the white of the eyes use one strand
of white and make two French knots by
twisting the thread twice around the
needle, see page 97.

TO MAKE UP

1. If you find the embroidery hoop too
small to fit over the T-shirt move the
frame as you stitch. If the T-shirt is very
small and you have difficulty fitting it on
the frame then you can unpick one side
seam, stretch the whole piece of cotton
over the hoop and re-sew the side seam
once the embroidery is completed.
Make sure that the T-shirt has straight
hems (and adjust them by sewing a new
hem if you need to), or the design may
end up on a slant.

2. First centre the design on the T-shirt,
measure carefully and use basting lines
as a positional guide, see page 93.
Position, pin and baste the interfacing
on the wrong side of the T-shirt front
and likewise the waste canvas, laying it
on the right side of the T-shirt front.
Position the hoop centrally around the
area to be stitched and then begin to
cross stitch, working through all three
layers: waste canvas on top, T-shirt in
the middle and interfacing underneath.

3. Remove the interfacing and waste
canvas (see page 90). Treat the finished
embroidery as described on page 94.

17

In the Tunnel Baseball Cap

The design on this cap was inspired by *The Sad Story of Henry*. Henry was afraid of the rain, so he stopped in a nice dry tunnel and refused to come out. "His driver and fireman argued with him, but he would not move. 'The rain will spoil my lovely green paint and red stripes,' he said. The guard blew his whistle till he had no more breath, and waved his flags till his arms ached; but Henry still stayed in the tunnel, and blew steam at him. 'I am

not going to spoil my lovely green paint and red stripes for you,' he said rudely. The passengers came and argued too, but Henry would not move. A fat director who was on the train told the guard to get a rope. 'We will pull you out,' he said. But Henry only blew steam at him and made him wet. They hooked the rope on and all pulled – except the fat director. 'My doctor has forbidden me to pull,' he said. They pulled and pulled and

pulled, but still Henry stayed in the tunnel. Then they tried pushing from the other end. The fat director said, 'One, two, three, push' ... but still Henry stayed in the tunnel. At last another train came. The guard waved his red flag and stopped it. The two engine drivers, the two firemen, and the two guards went and argued with Henry. 'Look, it has stopped raining,' they said. 'Yes, but it will begin again soon,' said Henry. 'And what would become of my green paint with red stripes then?' So they brought the other engine up, and it pushed and puffed and pushed as hard as ever it could. But still Henry stayed in the tunnel. So they gave it up. They told Henry, 'We shall leave you there for always and always and always.' They took up the old rails, built a wall in front of him, and cut a new tunnel. Now Henry can't get out, and he watches the trains rushing through the new tunnel..."

From *The Three Railway Engines* by The Rev. W. Awdry

A memorable scene showing Henry stuck in a tunnel (above left) and the original illustration reproduced on a baseball cap (opposite).

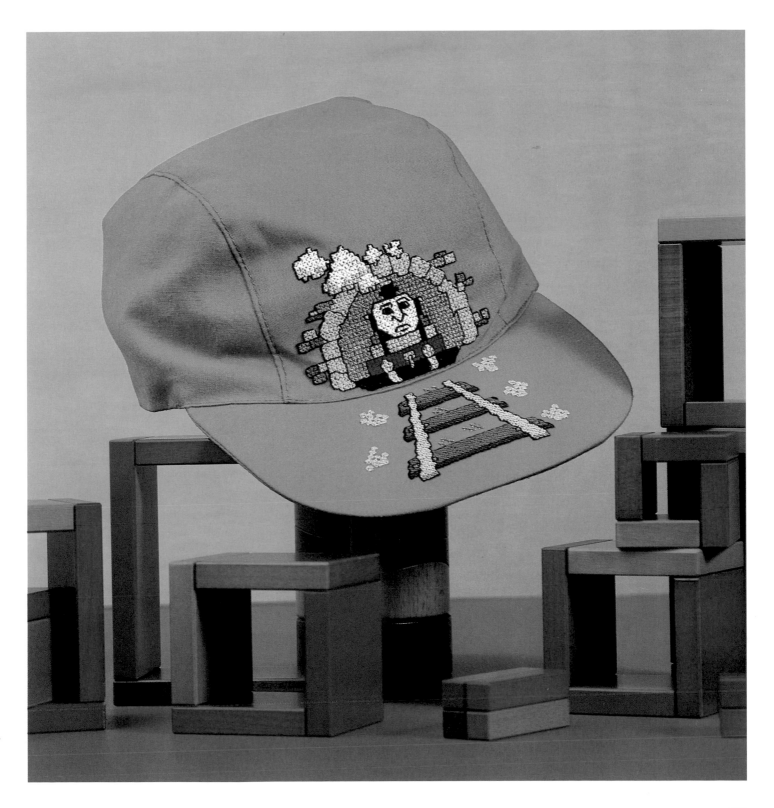

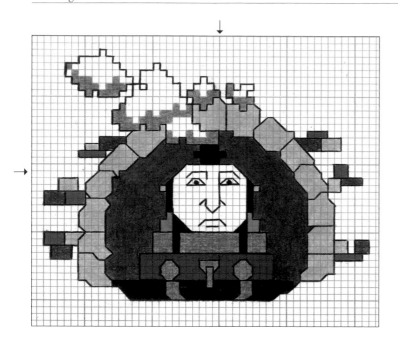

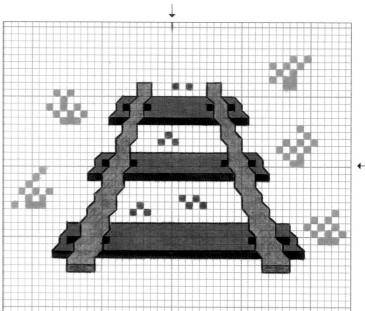

DMC	ANCHOR
Blanc	1
310	403
838	380
632	936
414	235
415	398
704	238
725	306
321	9046
700	228
437	362

ABILITY LEVEL: *Intermediate*

MEASUREMENTS

The actual design measures 13 x 20cm (5 x 8in). The cap will fit children aged between 5-12 years

MATERIALS

- Basic sewing kit (see page 92)
- Medium-weight green cotton fabric to measure 112.5 cm (45in) in width and 40cm (16in) in length
- One piece of interfacing, 15 x 25.5cm (6 x 10¼in)
- One piece of 14-count waste canvas, 15 x 25.5cm (6 x 10¼in)
- Fabric pen
- A 15cm (6in) embroidery hoop
- Stranded cotton, one skein of each of the colours shown in the key (left)
- Tapestry needle, size 24-26
- A pair of tweezers
- Calico or other lining of 90cm (36in) width, 15cm (6in) length
- Cream sewing thread
- A piece of stiff card, 18 x 13cm (7¼ x 5¼in)
- Green sewing thread
- A length of 0.5cm (¼in) wide elastic, 8.5cm (3¼in) long

TO EMBROIDER

Use two strands of thread for the cross stitch, see page 95. Use a single strand of black to outline the railway line, tunnel and train in backstitch, see page 95. Use two strands to backstitch the train's face in black. Use two strands of black and make a French knot for each eye by twisting the thread twice around the needle, see page 97. Use one strand of light gray to backstitch the outline of the clouds.

TO MAKE-UP

1. For the front panel of the cap (A), which shows Henry in the tunnel, first cut out a piece of green fabric 40 x 27.5cm (16 x 11in). To work out where to position the embroidery turn to the pattern shown on pages 98-9. Leave a margin of fabric below the embroidery area to stretch over the hoop. Mark the

dimension of the front panel (A) on the green fabric with a fabric pen. Then mark a vertical and horizontal line to establish the centre point of the design (see page 93) and highlight these lines with basting thread. Place the piece of interfacing under the position of the embroidery and the waste canvas on top; the stitching is worked through all three layers. Secure all three layers together with basting thread. Stretch the hoop over the fabric and begin stitching, starting at the centre point.

2. Follow the same principle for the railway track on the peak of the cap (B). This time however, cut out a piece of green fabric 25.5 x 25.5cm (10¼ x 10¼in) and position the embroidery according to pattern B on page 99.

3. When each piece of embroidery is complete, remove the hoop, interfacing and any excess waste canvas (see page 90) and treat as explained on page 94. Now you can start to sew the cap.

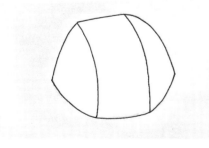

4. Make the lining first. Cut out pattern A once and pattern C twice in calico or other lining fabric, see page 98.

Pin and baste the rounded edge of each side panel (C) to a long straight edge of the front panel (A). Sew both seams by machine, trim away excess fabric and press. These pieces sewn together form a bowl shape.

5. Next, make the peak. Cut out pattern B, twice, see page 99. Note that one of these is already embroidered with the railway track. Place right sides together, pin and baste around the longer (outside) curved edge and sew by machine. Leave the inside curved edge open to insert the stiffening. Trim away any excess fabric, turn right side out and press. Cut out the template D on page 99 in card. Insert the card into the patterns B already sewn together and sew up the open edges as close to the card as possible so that the fabric is stretched tight over it.

6. Now sew the main cap. Cut out pattern A once (already embroidered) and pattern C twice in the green fabric, see page 98. Attach the piece of elastic across the short end of the front panel (A) which has no embroidery, ie at the back of the cap. Sew both ends of the

elastic firmly to the seam allowance on the wrong side of the fabric. Pin, baste and machine sew the curved sides of pattern C to a long straight edge of panel A, as for the calico lining; with right sides together. Press the seams towards the middle of the cap. Turn right side out and topstitch (see page 96) as close to the seam as possible.

7. Sew the peak to the front of the cap, lining up the embroidered designs. Fold in the raw edge of the front of the cap and carefully baste to the peak. Closely topstitch the two together.

8. Before you insert the lining, turn under the remaining raw edges of the cap, catching in the elastic at the back; pin, baste and topstitch a 1cm (⅜in) hem to hold the elastic in place. Topstitch allows the elastic to stretch.

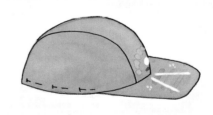

9. Finally place the calico lining inside the cap. Turn the raw edges under and pin, baste and sew to the main fabric using slipstitch, see page 96. Sew the lining inside the cap so that it will not be visible when the cap is worn.

Puffing James Pyjamas

The design on these pyjamas relates to the story *Leaves*, where James has to puff and pant a great deal to get up a hill and is eventually helped by Gordon who pushes from behind. "Now Autumn had come, and dead leaves fell. The wind usually puffed them away, but today rain made them heavy, and they did not move. The 'Home' signal showed 'clear', and James began to go faster. He started to climb the hill. 'I'll do it! I'll do it!' he puffed confidently. Half-way up he was not so sure! 'I *must* do it, I *must* do it,' he panted desperately, but try as he would, his wheels slipped on the leaves, and he couldn't pull the train at all. 'Whatsthematter? Whatsthematter?'

he gasped. 'Steady old boy, steady,' soothed his driver. His fireman put sand on the rails to help him grip; but James' wheels spun so fast that they only ground the sand and leaves to slippery mud, making things worse than before. The train slowly stopped. Then – 'Help! Help! Help!' whistled James; for though his wheels were turning forwards, the heavy coaches pulled him backwards, and the whole train started slipping down the hill. His driver shut off steam, carefully put on the brakes, and skilfully stopped the train... Gordon, who had followed with a goods train, saw what had happened. Gordon left his trucks, and crossed over to James. 'I thought you could climb hills,' he chuckled. James didn't answer; he had no steam! 'Ah well! We live and learn,' said Gordon, 'we live and learn. Never mind, little James,' he went on kindly, 'I'm going to push behind. Whistle when you're ready.' James waited till he had plenty of steam, then 'Peep! Peep!' he called. 'Poop! Poop! Poop!' 'Pull hard,' puffed Gordon. 'We'll do it !' puffed James.

From *Gordon the Big Engine* by The Rev. W. Awdry

James puffing through the countryside (above left) and James stitched onto a pair of pyjamas (opposite).

FOR THE RIGHT COLLAR

	DMC	ANCHOR
■	310	403
■	518	168
■	321	9046
■	451	233
■	725	306

FOR THE LEFT COLLAR

	DMC	ANCHOR
☐	Blanc	1
■	310	403
■	518	168
■	321	9046
■	451	233

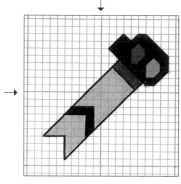

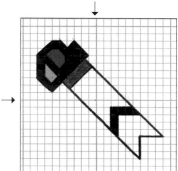

FOR THE POCKET

	DMC	ANCHOR
■	825	162
■	700	228
■	321	9046
■	632	936
☐	Blanc	1
■	310	403
■	758	868

FOR THE TROUSERS

	DMC	ANCHOR		DMC	ANCHOR
■	321	9046	■	415	398
☐	Blanc	1	■	632	936
■	310	403	■	436	363
■	451	233	■	725	306

ABILITY LEVEL: *Intermediate*

MEASUREMENTS

The cross stitch design on the collar
measures 3 x 3cm (1¼ x 1¼in); the
pocket design measures 7.5 x 5cm (3 x 2in)
and the design on the trousers measures
12 x 6cm (4¾ x 2⅜in)

MATERIALS

• Basic sewing kit (see page 92)
• Stranded cotton, one skein of each of the
  colours shown in the keys (left)
• Tapestry needle, size 24-26

For the collar

• A 10cm (4in) embroidery hoop
• Two pieces of interfacing, each one
  measuring 6 x 6cm (2⅜ x 2⅜in)
• Two pieces of 14-count waste canvas, each
  measuring 6 x 6cm (2⅜ x 2⅜in)
• A pair of tweezers
• Two pieces of cotton or calico, each one
  measuring 9 x 9cm (3⅝ x 3⅝in)

For the pocket

• A 10cm (4in) embroidery hoop
• One piece of interfacing, measuring 15 x
  15cm (6 x 6in)
• One piece of 14-count waste canvas
  measuring 8 x 8cm (3¼ x3¼in)

For the trousers

• A 10cm (4in) embroidery hoop
• Two pieces of interfacing, each one
  measuring 20 x 12cm (8 x 4¼in)
• Two pieces of 14-count waste canvas, each
  one measuring 20 x 12cm (8 x 4¾in)

TO EMBROIDER

FOR THE COLLAR: use two strands for the
cross stitch, see page 95. Outline the
designs using a single strand of black in
backstitch, see page 95.

1. To embroider the collar of a ready-
made pair of pyjamas, first pin and baste
the two pieces of calico behind the
wings of the collar so that you can stretch
the hoop over the collar before you start
to embroider.

2. Now work out where to position the
embroidery on the collar. To do this centre the designs on the area that is available using a vertical and a horizontal line
of basting to act as a guide, see page 93.
Pin and baste one piece of interfacing
under the collar and one piece of waste
canvas over the collar, making sure that

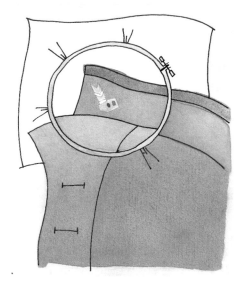

these are positioned to align with the
basting guidelines already made. Fix the
hoop and start to embroider. Repeat for
the other wing of the collar. Treat the
finished embroidery as described on
page 94.

FOR THE POCKET: use two strands for the cross stitch, see page 95. Outline the shoes using a single strand of white in backstitch, see page 95. Outline the rest of the design using a single strand of black in backstitch. For the eyes and buttons use one strand to make a French knot by twisting the yarn twice around the needle, see page 97. For the ears make a French knot with one twist around the needle.

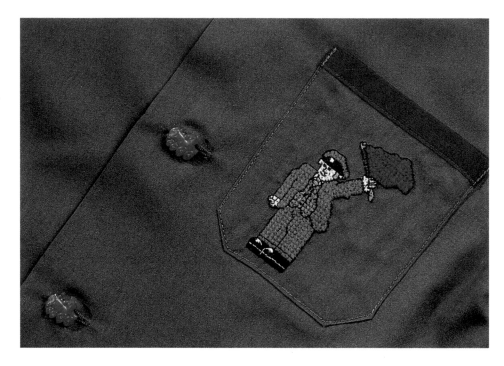

1. The only way you can embroider on the pocket of ready-made pyjamas is to carefully unpick the seams and remove the pocket. Press the turnings of the unpicked pocket flat and pin and baste the wrong side of the pocket to the piece of interfacing.

2. Centre the design on the pocket inside the unpicked seam lines, see page 93. Place the piece of waste canvas on the right side of the pocket and use the basting lines to centre the design. Pin and baste all three layers (Interfacing, pocket and waste canvas) together. Mark "top" of pocket on the waste canvas so you do not embroider the design upside-down! Fix the hoop and start to embroider. Treat the finished embroidery, see page 94.

3. Press the turnings of the pocket back under into their original folds, Then pin, baste and machine-sew the pocket back in place onto the pyjama top. To make the pyjamas that extra bit special remove the ordinary buttons and replace them with novelty train buttons to match the colours in the embroidery design.

FOR THE PYJAMA BOTTOMS: use two strands for the cross stitch. Outline the smoke in a single strand in backstitch. Outline the face using two strands in backstitch and the rest of the design in a single strand in backstitch.

1. Lay the pyjama bottoms flat. Baste a vertical line of stitches on the outside edge of each leg as a guideline for positioning the design. Unpick the inside seam of each pyjama leg to about one-third of the way up so that the trouser bottoms open out to give you room to position the design.

The next step is to baste two parallel lines of horizontal stitches around the base of each pyjama leg, approximately 4cm (1⅜in) up from the bottom hem of the trousers. These lines will serve as positional guides for the embroidery, see page 93.

3. When the embroidery is complete you can sew up the unpicked seams of the inside trouser legs and sew up around the hem where necessary. Then place a novelty button on the waist band to match the buttons on the pyjama top to make them all of a piece.

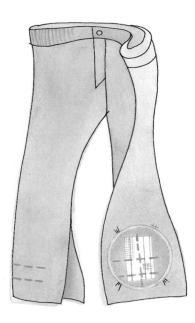

2. Pin a piece of interfacing on the wrong side of the pyjama fabric, following the basting guidelines made in the previous step. Next pin a piece of waste canvas on the right side of the pyjama fabric and baste all three layers together. Fix the hoop centrally over the area that is to be stitched and then start to embroider working outward from the centre. Repeat for the opposite pyjama leg, making sure that the two designs are symmetrical and aligned properly. Treat the finished embroidery.

Stop and Go Slippers

The designs on my stop and go slippers are a reminder of the story *Mind that Bike!* "One day a man came from the station office to tell Tom that some papers needed signing. 'Oh dear,' he said anxiously. 'This is going to make me very late.' He asked Percy to keep an eye on his bicycle while he was gone, and propped it carefully against the fence near the platform ramp. He was gone a long time, and had not returned when Percy was

ready to go. Some boys were playing on the platform and Percy was worried. 'Sorry Percy,' said his driver. 'We must be off – time and the Fat Controller wait for no man.' In the flurry of starting, no-one noticed that one of the boys had picked up Tom's bicycle. He pedalled too far along the platform, and before he could stop, ran out of control down the ramp. He reached the bottom just as Percy started away. Fortunately the boy fell clear in time, but the bicycle swerved beneath Percy's wheels and disappeared with a crunch. Percy's driver stopped the train quickly, and they extracted the remains, but the red bicycle was beyond repair. Tom came running, and he, the driver, the station master and the guard all told the boys what Bad Boys they were. 'I'm sorry Mr. Tipper,' apologised Percy. 'Never mind, Percy,' said the postman. 'It wasn't your fault, and I never liked that bike much anyway.' When the Fat Controller heard about the accident he ordered that Tom should be provided with a new bicycle at once. But next morning, when Percy arrived at Ffarquhar he saw a brand new red van standing in the yard, beside the ruins of the bicycle. Close by stood Tom Tipper, beaming from ear to ear. 'That accident did me a good turn, Percy,' he smiled, 'and now my chief has decided to let me have a new van after all.'"

From *Really Useful Engines* by The Rev. W. Awdry

Percy smiling at Mr Tipper's new van (above right); a pair of soft felt slippers (opposite).

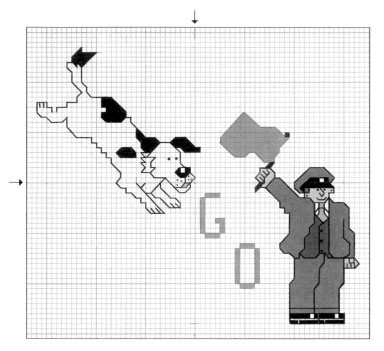

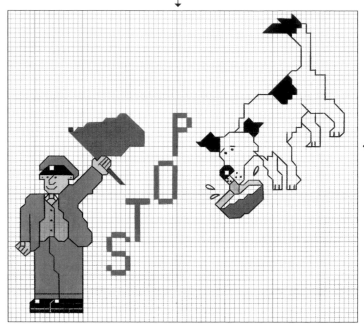

FOR THE GUARDS

	DMC	ANCHOR
▨	825	162
▨	700	228
▨	321	9046
▨	632	936
☐	Blanc	1
■	310	403
▨	760	9

FOR THE DOGS

	DMC	ANCHOR
☐	Blanc	1
■	310	403
▨	758	868
▨	321	9046
▨	436	363

MEASUREMENTS

The cross stitch designs both measure 14 x 6cm (5⅝ x 2⅜in)

ABILITY LEVEL: *Advanced*

MATERIALS

- Basic sewing kit (see page 92)
- Two pieces of touch-and-close fastening, 5.8 x 2cm (2¼ x ¾in)
- Two pieces of 14-count waste canvas, 17 x 20cm (6¾ x 8in)
- Two pieces of interfacing, 17 x 20cm (6¾ x 8in)
- Stranded cotton, one skein of each of the colours shown in the keys (left)
- Tapestry needle, size 24-26
- A 15cm (6in) embroidery hoop
- A pair of tweezers
- Piece of navy felt, 26 x 84cm (10⅜ x 33⅝in)
- Piece of yellow felt, 26 x 84cm (10⅜ x 33⅝in)
- Piece of red felt, 26 x 84cm (10⅜ x 33⅝in)
- Two strands of red Paterna wool No. 970
- A of sheepskin, 20.5 x 23cm (8¼ x 9¼in)
- A leather hole puncher
- A needle with a triangular tip, for leather

TO EMBROIDER

For both slippers: use two strands for the cross stitch, see page 95. Outline the whole of each design using one strand of black working in backstitch, see page 95. Outline the red lettering "stop" and the green lettering "go" in a single strand of backstitch. Use one strand of black for the guard's and the dog's eyes, and the buttons on the guard's waistcoat: for all these make French knots by twisting the yarn twice around the needle, see page 97. For the guard's ears and the dog's whiskers again make French knots, this time twisting the yarn only once around the needle. To embroider the white shoes use a single strand and work in backstitch. And for the milk drops on the slipper for the left foot use two strands and work in chain stitch, see page 97.

TO MAKE UP

1. To start the cross stitch, work the right foot first. Trace the pattern A for the right foot (see page 100-101) onto a piece of yellow felt measuring 25 x 40cm (10 x 16in); do not cut out.

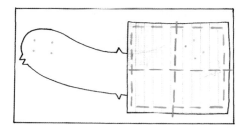

2. Use tailor's tacks (see page 96) to mark aligning points on pattern A, see pages 100-101. These points mark the middle of the shoe, the centrepoint at the front and the area where touch-and-close strips will later be placed (see step 7).

3. Use basting lines to position the embroidery correctly (see the illustration above), also refer to pattern A on pages 100-101. Place one piece of waste canvas centrally over the basting lines, which act as a positional guide.

4. Place one piece of interfacing below the layer of felt and directly underneath the position of the waste canvas. Pin and baste all three layers together. Fix the hoop and start to embroider. Repeat the same process for the left foot, following pattern B on pages 100-101. Treat the finished embroidery as described on page 94. Do not wash the felt or it will lose its soft texture and be ruined.

5. To start making up the slippers, cut out patterns A and B (the two pieces of yellow felt already embroidered). Next, cut out patterns A and B in red felt for the lining, see pages 100-101. Cut out pattern C in navy felt four times to edge the slippers, see page 100. Cut out pattern D twice in sheepskin for the soles, see page 101. You must reverse the pattern for a left and a right sole.

6. Punch holes all around the edge of the soles about 0.7mm (¼in) apart.

7. Work the right slipper first. Pin and machine stitch one side of a strip of touch-and-close to the area indicated on pattern B of the red lining. Pin and stitch the other side of the same strip of touch-and-close to the area shown on pattern A of the yellow felt through two layers of fabric, see pages 100-101. Once the slipper is folded along the middle line indicated by tailor's tacks on patterns A and B, the pieces of touch-and-close will align, to give the slipper its shape.

8. Pin and baste the yellow embroidered pattern A to the lining pattern B all around the edge. Blanket stitch (see page 97) around the top edge of the slipper from centre point to centre point, as shown by tailor's tacks on pattern A (see the illustration in the top right-hand corner). Next pin the two centre points together, secure the aligning strips of touch-and-close, and baste to join so that the slipper takes on its shape.

9. Pin and baste two long narrow strips of navy felt together (cut from pattern C) so that they form a double thickness. Baste the short ends of the joined strips together to form a circle and hide this short section of basting with a few blanket stitches. Remove the basting.

10. Then take the circle of navy felt and pin and baste it all around the base of the slipper. Conceal and secure the basting stitches with blanket stitch. Remove the basting after blanket stitching.

11. Pin and baste the bottom edge of the navy strip to the right sole. You can trim away some of the sheepskin fur around the edge of the sole to make sewing easier. Sew a few hand stitches through some punched holes around the sole to keep it in place. Blanket stitch the bottom edge of the navy strip to the sole. Repeat steps 5 to 11 for the left slipper.

Thomas and Clarabel Scarf

A warm winter scarf is made all the more attractive with Thomas and his beloved coach Clarabel stitched onto a bright-red background, the motifs are taken from the story *Thomas and the Guard*. "Thomas the tank engine is very proud of his branch line. He thinks it is the most important part of the whole railway. He has two coaches. They are old, and need new paint, but he loves them very much. He calls them Annie and Clarabel. Annie can only take passengers, but Clarabel can take passengers, luggage and the guard. As they run backwards and forwards along the line, Thomas sings them little songs, and Annie and Clarabel sing too. When Thomas starts from a station he sings, 'Oh, come along! We're rather late, Oh, come along! We're rather late.' And the coaches sing, 'We're coming along, we're coming along.' They don't mind what Thomas says to them because they know he is trying to please the Fat Controller; and they know, too, that if Thomas is cross, he is not cross with them. He is cross with the engines on the main line who have made him late.

"One day they had to wait for Henry's train. It was late. Thomas was getting crosser and crosser. 'How can I run my line properly if Henry is always late? He doesn't realize that the Fat Controller depends on ME,' and he

whistled impatiently. At last Henry came. 'Where have you been, lazy-bones?' asked Thomas crossly. 'Oh dear, my system is out of order; no one understands my case. You don't know what I suffer,' moaned Henry. 'Rubbish!' said Thomas, 'you're too fat; you need exercise!'"

From *Tank Engine Thomas Again*, by The Rev. W. Awdry

Thomas pulling his favourite passenger coaches, Annie and Clarabel (above right). Here an ordinary scarf worn by a teddy bear has been transformed by adding Thomas and Clarabel in cross stitch on either end.

FOR CLARABEL

	DMC	ANCHOR
	415	398
	356	5975
	498	43
	Blanc	1
	310	403
	725	306
	437	362
	760	9

FOR THOMAS

	DMC	ANCHOR
	760	9
	824	164
	415	398
	725	306
	321	9046
	310	403
	Blanc	1

ABILITY LEVEL: *Easy*

MEASUREMENTS

The Clarabel design measures 5 x 8.5cm (2 x 3⅜in) and the Thomas design measures 6.5 x 8cm (2⅝ x 3¼in)

MATERIALS

- Basic sewing kit (see page 92)
- One soft, plain red scarf
- Two pieces of 14-count waste canvas; one 12 x 12cm (4¾ x 4¾in); the other 9 x 12cm (3½ x 4¾in)
- Two pieces of interfacing; one 12 x 12cm (4¾ x 4¾ in); the other 9 x 12cm (3½ x 4¾in)
- A 15cm (6in) embroidery hoop
- Stranded cotton, one skein of each of the colours shown in the keys (left)
- Tapestry needle, size 24-26
- A pair of tweezers

TO EMBROIDER

Use two strands from the skein for the cross stitch, see page 95. The eyes are formed with French knots that are made with two strands twisted twice around the needle, see page 97. To make the outline around both trains and the hearts

work one strand of black in backstitch, see page 95. Outline the faces in backstitch using two strands of black. Backstitch around the smoke in gray; backstitch the red train markings with two strands of red and backstitch with two strands of yellow around the windows and the number 1.

TO MAKE UP

1. First centre the two designs on the waste canvas; measure carefully and use basting lines as a positional guide, see page 93. Next decide where exactly on the scarf you want to position the two train motifs; I decided to place them approximately 5cm (2in) in from either end of the scarf. Make sure the designs are symmetrically placed. Here the stitching is worked through three layers; the top layer is the waste canvas, the middle layer is the tear-away interfacing and the third layer is the scarf itself. For directions on how to stitch onto a backing (in this case the scarf) using waste canvas and interfacing, see page 90.

2. Once the canvas and interfacing have been basted in position fix the embroidery hoop and begin to cross stitch.

3. To finish, you need to remove the waste canvas and interfacing – for instructions see page 90.

Terence and Bertie Dungarees

The tractor called Terence comes into the story *Thomas, Terence and the Snow*. "As Thomas puffed along, he heard the 'chug chug chug' of a tractor at work. One day, stopping for a signal, he saw the tractor close by. 'Hullo!' said the tractor, 'I'm Terence; I'm ploughing.' 'I'm Thomas; I'm pulling a train. What ugly wheels you've got.' 'They're not ugly, they're caterpillars,' said Terence. 'I can go anywhere; I don't need rails.' Later on in the same story Thomas gets stuck in a snowdrift (see page 58) and Terence comes to his rescue.

Bertie the bus appears in the story *Thomas and Bertie*. "One day Thomas was waiting at the junction, when a bus

came into the yard. 'Hullo!' said Thomas, 'Who are you?' 'I'm Bertie, who are you?' 'I'm Thomas; I run this line.' 'So you're Thomas. Ah – I remember now, you stuck in the snow, I took your passengers and Terence pulled you out. I've come to help you with your passengers today.' 'Help me!' said Thomas crossly, going bluer than ever and letting off steam. 'I can go faster than you.' 'You can't.' 'I can.' 'I'll race you,' said Bertie. Their drivers agreed. The station master said, 'Are you ready? – Go!' and they were off. Thomas never could go fast at first, and Bertie drew in front. Thomas was running well but he did not hurry. 'Why don't you go fast? Why don't you go fast?' called Annie and Clarabel anxiously. 'Wait and see, wait and see,' hissed Thomas. 'He's a long way ahead, a long way ahead,' they wailed, but Thomas didn't mind. He remembered the Level Crossing. There was Bertie fuming at the gates while they sailed gaily through. 'Goodbye, Bertie,' called Thomas."

From *Tank Engine Thomas Again* by The Rev. W. Awdry

Thomas and Bertie decide on a race (above left). Dress up a pair of dungarees with Terence and Bertie (opposite).

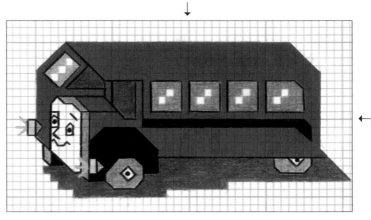

FOR THE TRACTOR AND BUS

	DMC	ANCHOR
☐	Blanc	1
■	310	403
■	321	9046
■	414	235
■	415	398
■	725	306
■	758	868
■	3052	859
■	632	936

ABILITY LEVEL: *Intermediate*

MEASUREMENTS

The tractor design measures 3.5 x 6.5cm (1⅜ x 2⅝in) and the bus design measures 3 x 7cm (1¼ x 2¾in)

MATERIALS

- Basic sewing kit (see page 92)
- One piece of 16-count Aida, in white (measure this according to the dimensions of the dungaree pockets; refer to the instructions on how to make up)
- Stranded cotton, one skein of each of the colours shown in the key (above)

- Tapestry needle, size 24-26
- A 15cm (6in) embroidery hoop
- One pair of size 2-3 year old's dungarees
- Three lengths of red bias binding, 4cm (1⅝in) wide (see the instructions on how to make up)
- One length of green bias binding, 4cm (1⅝in) wide (refer to the instructions on how to make up)

TO EMBROIDER

Use two strands to work the cross stitch, see page 95. For the tractor: use two strands to work the steering wheel, face and funnel in backstitch, see page 95. Outline in a single strand. For the eyes, use two strands to make French knots with two twists around the needle, see page 97. For the bus: outline the top of the bus in a single strand of red and the bottom in a single strand of black in backstitch. Outline the lamps using two strands in backstitch. Work the face in two strands in backstitch. Outline the rest of the design in a single strand in backstitch. For the eyes make two French knots using two strands with two twists around the needle.

TO MAKE UP

1. The shape of the piece of Aida that you will embroider depends on the particular style of the dungarees that you have purchased, and must be cut out accordingly. Whatever shape of pocket you have, cut out the Aida larger all round than the pocket shape and give it a generous margin so that the piece is large enough to fit onto an embroidery hoop. Work out where you wish to place the design on the pocket. Centre the design on the Aida; measure with care and use basting lines as a positional guide, see page 93. Fix the hoop in the middle of the area to be stitched and start to cross stitch. Treat the finished embroidery as described on page 94.

2. Cut out the shape of the pocket in the embroidered Aida. Here the pocket is a half-circle shape sitting on the bib of the dungarees. If your dungarees have different-shaped pockets, or if you prefer to embroider the side, or rear pockets then you must cut out and position the designs accordingly.

3. Dungarees vary in the way they are sewn, but follow the basic principles for this project from the method given below. Unpick the bib pocket from the dungarees, opening the horizontal adjoining seam underneath the pocket.

4. Pin and baste the two quarter circles of embroidered Aida in position on the right side of the pocket. Measure and cut three lengths of red bias binding with an extra 2.5cm (1in) at each end: one the length of the curve of the pocket (A); one the length of the straight bottom edge (B); one the height of the pocket (C). Cut a length of green binding the length of the bottom edge (B).

5. Turn in the long edges of strip C by 1cm (⅜in). Pin, baste and machine stitch the strip down the middle of the pocket to divide it in two; the turned in edges of the bias strip should hide the raw edges of the straight side of each piece of embroidery. Cut away any excess bias top and bottom.

6. Attach the bias strip A to the outside curve of the pocket in the same way: machine stitch on the right side of the

pocket, fold the bias over and oversew on the wrong side (see page 96).

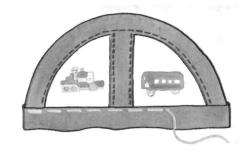

7. Attach the bias strip B to the bottom edge of the pocket in the same way: machine stitch on the right side of the pocket and leave the other edge of binding raw. Fold in the raw short ends to neaten the corners.

8. Take the length of green bias binding (B). Fold in the raw short ends to the length of the bottom edge of the pocket. Fold in half lengthways and press.

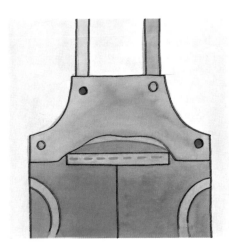

9. Pin and baste the green bias strip onto the lower side of the horizontal seam opened in step 3.

10. Insert the straight bottom edge of the pocket into the seam opening and align the corners of the green and red bias strips. Pin and baste so that all is neatly aligned: the green bias strip should show about 0.5cm (¼in) below the red, which shows about 1cm (⅜in), when the pocket is in position. Machine stitch in place.

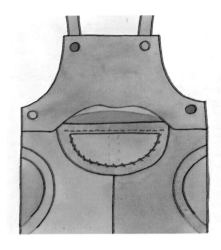

11. Topstitch (see page 96) the trousers and the bib of the dungarees together again to close up the seam.

12. Turn the pocket up and pin and baste it back into its original position on the bib of the dungarees. Machine stitch in place, making a neat line of reversing stitches at three points around the curved edge of the pocket so that it is really secure. All the bias binding should be about 1cm (⅜in) wide on the finished pocket. You can also add matching strips of bias binding to the hip pockets, rear pockets and trouser cuffs to make the dungarees all of a piece.

Henry Baby's Bib

One of the most memorable stories about Henry is called *Henry's Sneeze*. "One lovely Saturday morning, Henry was puffing along. The sun shone, the fields were green, the birds sang; Henry had plenty of steam in his boiler, and he was feeling happy. 'I feel so well, I feel so well,' he sang. 'Trickety trock, trickety trock,' hummed his coaches. Henry saw some boys on a bridge. 'Peep! Peep! Hullo!' he whistled cheerfully. 'Peep! Peep! Peeeep!' he called the next moment. 'Oh! Oh! Oooh!' For the boys didn't wave and take his number; they dropped stones on him instead... They stopped the train and the guard asked if any passengers were hurt. No one was hurt but

everyone was cross. They saw the fireman's bumped head, and told him what to do for it, and they looked at Henry's paint. 'Call the police,' they shouted angrily. 'No!' said the driver, 'leave it to Henry and me. We'll teach those lads a lesson.' 'What will you do?' they asked. 'Can you keep a secret?' 'Yes, yes,' they all said. 'Well then,' said the driver, 'Henry is going to sneeze at them... The guard's flag waved, his whistle blew, and they were off. Soon in the distance they saw the bridge. There were the boys, and they all had stones. 'Are you ready, Henry?' said his driver. 'Sneeze hard when I tell you.' 'Now!' he said, and turned the handle. "Atisha Atisha Atishooooooh!' Smoke and steam and ashes spouted from his funnel. They went all over the bridge, and all over the boys who ran away as black as soot. 'Well done, Henry,' laughed his driver, 'they won't drop stones on engines again.'"

From *Henry the Green Engine* by The Rev. W. Awdry

The piglets – and smiling Henry – look happy and well-fed on this baby's bib (opposite). An original illustration from the memorable story where Henry gets his revenge by sneezing over some naughty boys (above).

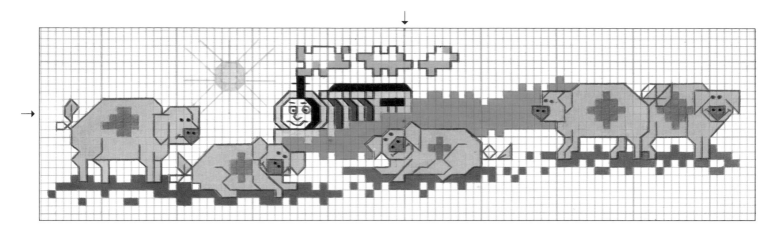

	DMC	ANCHOR
■	356	5975
▨	754	4146
▨	415	398
■	414	235
▨	704	238
■	700	228
▨	725	306
■	760	9
■	321	9046
■	310	403
□	Blanc	1

ABILITY LEVEL: *Intermediate*

MEASUREMENTS

The actual design measures 13 x 3cm (5¼ x 1¼in)

MATERIALS

• Basic sewing kit (see page 92)
• One piece of 18-count Aida, 24 x 28cm (9⅝ x 11¼in), in white
• Stranded cotton, one skein of each of the colours shown in the key (left)
• Tapestry needle, size 24-26
• A 15cm (6in) embroidery hoop
• One piece of soft, white towelling, 24 x 28cm (9⅝ x 11¼in)
• Length of bias binding, 1.5m (60in) long, 2.5cm (1in) wide, in yellow

TO MAKE UP

Working on 18-count Aida, use a single strand for the cross stitch, see page 95. Outline the pigs, the train, the smoke and the sun with one strand working in backstitch, see page 95. Work the pigs' faces (including the eyes and the nostrels) as well as the face of the train in a single strand working in backstitch. For the eyes of the train make two French knots, twisting a single strand just once

around the needle, see page 97. Note that if you choose to work on a coarser 16-count Aida then you should use two strands of yarn for the cross stitch.

TO MAKE UP

1. Lightly mark out the pattern of the bib (see page 102) onto the piece of Aida using a fabric marker or a pencil. Centre the design on the Aida; measure carefully and use basting lines as a positional guide, see page 93. I started the design approximately 3.5cm (1⅜in) above the bottom edge of the bib. Fix the embroidery hoop in the middle of the area to be stitched and start to cross stitch working from the centre outwards. Treat the finished embroidery as described on page 94.

2. To make the bib, cut out the embroidered Aida according to the pattern shown on page 102. Cut out the same pattern in the towelling. Cut the strip of bias binding into two lengths: one 76cm (30⅜in) and the other 74cm (29⅝in) long.

3. Pin the Aida and towelling wrong sides together, baste all round the edge to make the Aida and towelling a piece.

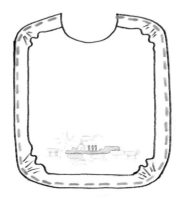

4. Fold one side of the longer strip of bias binding lengthways and baste it all around the edge of the bib so that it hides the raw edges; machine stitch down. Fold in the raw edge of the binding on the other side of the bib, tuck under, pin, baste and hand sew so that the binding is finally about 1cm (⅜in) wide on each side of the bib.

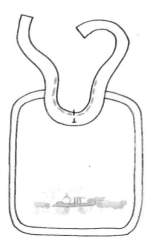

5. Fold the shorter strip of bias binding which is used to trim the neck edge. Measure the length and find the middle of the strip; mark this point and pin it to the centre of the curve of the neck, on the front of the bib. Next pin and baste the binding around the inside curve of the neck and machine sew carefully in place. To neaten the ties to tie the bib, fold the binding in half lengthways, tuck in both raw edges by a just few millime-

tres, pin, baste and slipstitch to finish (see page 96). Tuck in the open ends of each tie and finish with just a few neat hand stitches. Because a bib is used at feeding times this item will need to be washed frequently, however the yarns for the cross stitch are colourfast so washing at a low temperature will not damage the design. Dry the bib flat on a towel to prevent the cross stitch becoming distorted.

43

Gifts

Making gifts for your friends and family is very rewarding, both for the recipient and for yourself. The projects in this chapter are pitched across all levels of ability. The Christmas card, the birthday card and the key ring are designed for novices. A good haberdashery should stock the basic card and key ring kits needed. The cake band is only a little more complicated and is a delightful way to dress up a cake for all kinds of celebrations. The Fat Controller, one of the most memorable characters created by the Reverend W. Awdry, features on the bookmark design, which is both easy to make and the perfect marker for *Thomas the Tank Engine* books. The drawstring purse requires some sewing at an intermediate level and makes a charming gift, useful for storing trinkets and treasures. The pencil case requires some careful sewing but it is small in scale and inexpensive to make – any child would surely be proud to take it to school. Feel free to adapt any other cross stitch designs in the book as well as varying the colours to the projects that are featured here.

Above This picture of Thomas stuck in a snowdrift comes from the story *Thomas, Terence and the Snow*. The story inspired my Christmas card design on page 58.
Opposite A selection of the cross stitch items you can make as gifts – including a pencil case on the left, a bookmark below it, a drawstring purse on the right and a Christmas card above.

Thomas Pencil Case

The pencil case shown opposite relates to the story *Drip-Tank* where Thomas springs a leak. "Next day Henry's train was late at the junction. When Thomas set out along the valley he was trying to make up for lost time. Suddenly there was a loud bang, and something hard hit the bottom of his left-hand watertank. 'Ouch!' exclaimed Thomas, and stopped. As he did so he felt water splashing cold against his wheels. 'One of your siderods has broken,' said his driver. 'It swung up and punctured your tank – we'll have to get help.' At Ffarquhar,

Percy was shunting. The station-master came up. 'Leave those trucks please, Percy,' he said. 'Thomas has got a hole in his watertank – there's water dripping everywhere, and he can't get home on his own.' Percy was still cross with Thomas. 'I won't go,' he said. 'Thomas called me a drip – let him jolly well stay there and drip himself.' 'But what about Annie and Clarabel and the passengers?' reminded Percy's driver. 'Do they deserve to stay out all night too?' Percy was

sorry at once. 'I forgot them,' he said. 'We must rescue them in case they turn into drips too.' He hurried away. He found Thomas near the river. Everyone was glad to see him, and the passengers thanked him for coming. 'I'm sorry I was rude,' said Thomas, as Percy helped him back to the shed. 'That tank of mine turned me into a bigger drip than we expected, didn't it? Can we be friends again, please?' Percy was delighted to agree."

From *More About Thomas the Tank Engine* by The Rev. W. Awdry

In the story Drip-Tank, poor old Thomas finds a hole in his watertank and has to be rescued by Percy (above right). The original illustration is translated into cross stitch and made up into a useful pencil case (opposite).

FOR THE TRAIN

PATERNA WOOL

⬜	A712 (3 skeins)
⬛	A220
⬛	A422
⬛	A871
⬛	A970
⬛	A552
⬛	A540
⬛	A553
⬛	A256
⬜	A260
⬛	A201
⬛	A825

ABILITY LEVEL: *Intermediate*

MEASUREMENTS

The finished cross stitch design measures 16 x 8.5cm (6⅜ x 3⅜in)

MATERIALS

- Basic sewing kit (see page 92)
- One piece of 14-count plastic canvas, 20 x 28cm (8 x 11¼in), in white
- Skeins of Paterna 100 per cent wool in the colours shown in the key (above)
- Tapestry needle, size 20
- Green cotton fabric of 112.5cm (45in) width, 30cm (12in) long
- Green sewing thread to match above fabric
- Two paper clips
- Touch-and-close fastening, 20cm (8in) long
- Two lengths of elastic, 0.5cm (¼in) wide; each 6cm (2⅜in) long
- Four yellow wooden beads
- One skein of black stranded cotton (DMC no. 310 or Anchor no. 403)

TO EMBROIDER

For the yellow background work in half cross stitch, see page 95. Because this project has a mass of yellow background stitches, try to work these in neat, even stitches so that you end up with an even overall texture. Half cross stitch is an economical stitch and you may not use up all three skeins of wool. Because the yarn used in this project is thicker than the stranded cotton used in the other projects in the book, work with a single thread of wool. However, use three strands of the black DMC stranded cotton for the details on the face of the train, the guard and the guard's suit; for the detail on the train work in backstitch, see page 95.

TO MAKE UP

1. Take a piece of plastic mesh canvas and measure to a point 16cm (6⅜in) down each longer edge – this section is your embroidery area. Follow pattern A on pages 104-105 and mark the vertical and horizontal lines shown on page 104 to centre the design; use a biro for this, or baste the lines if you wish. Work the embroidery design in half cross stitch, see page 95.

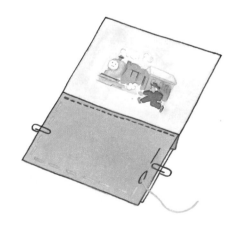

2. Cover the remaining plastic canvas with a piece of green fabric cut out according to pattern B on page 104.

Where the pattern indicates a 1cm (⅜in) seam allowance (as a seam line) press down with an iron and lay the fold along the last row of half cross stitch; keep in place with paper clips. Baste along the fold before sewing by hand in backstitch (see page 95); make a stitch in each hole of the underlying canvas. Baste the remaining three sides of the green fabric to the canvas, leaving the raw edges showing.

3. Cut out another piece of green fabric which should be 4cm (1⅜in) larger than the plastic mesh, see pattern C on page 105; this forms the lining for the pencil case. Cut a strip of touch-and-close 20cm (8in) long.

4. Cut out four strips of green fabric following pattern D on page 104. Cut on the straight grain. Each strip measures 4 x 32cm (1⅝ x 12¼in) and will form the ties. Turn in the raw edges of each strip lengthwise by 0.5cm (¼in) and press. Fold each strip in half lengthwise, pin, baste and machine stitch close to the edge. Each finished strip should be 1cm (⅜in) wide.

5. Position the ties 5cm (2in) in from the outside top edge of the embroidered section, pin and baste to the right side of the embroidery.

6. Place the green lining panel (C) over the positioned ties; pin, baste and make a seam with the sewing machine 0.5cm (¼in) below the top edge of the plastic canvas (about three lines of mesh down). Keep the sewing along one line of the mesh. Turn the lining (C) over the top of the mesh so it lies against the back of the embroidery.

7. Attach the remaining two ties to the opposite end of the pencil case on the right side of the bottom edge. Turn under 0.5cm (¼in) of the raw edge of the lining piece (C) and pin, baste and machine sew over the secured ends of the second pair of ties, as before. The green lining should just be visible on both short ends of the pencil case on the embroidery (right) side. Baste the lining (C) down each long edge of the pencil case.

8. Turn the pencil case wrong side (lining side) up and position the strips of touch-and-close just inside the top and

bottom edges so that it just overlaps the seams already running on the reverse (right) side. Pin and baste in place. To secure the strip of touch-and-close at the bottom edge of the pencil case work two parallel lines of topstitch, see page 96. To secure the strip at the top edge, work a line of topstitch sewing from the right side of the pencil case along the top of the touch-and-close strip and slipstitch (see page 96) along the lower parallel edge of the same strip so that the stitches do not show through on the right side.

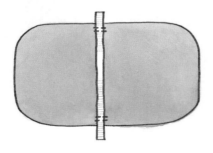

9. To make up the sides of the pencil case cut out two strips of bias binding from the green fabric, following pattern E on page 105. Each one measures 4 x 32cm (1⅝ x 12¾in). For the side panels also using the green fabric, cut out two of pattern F on page 105. Also cut two strips of 0.5cm (¼in) wide elastic, 6cm (2⅜in) long. Stretch and pin a length of elastic to the "tunnelling area" marked by a broken line along the straight edge on pattern F. Secure each end of the elastic by machine, reversing over the stitching several times.

10. Fold the side panels in half, pin, baste and make a seam by machine to form a "tunnel" around the elastic. Baste all around the edge of each panel and gather the bottom into a curve with loose basting or "easing" stitches, see page 95.

11. Place a binding strip (E) down each long edge on the right side of the pencil case: pin, baste and sew in place. Before turning the binding in to neaten up the edges of the pencil case, sew in the side panels. Pin and baste the side panels to the pencil case, just below the strips of touch-and-close; leave the raw edges on the outside of the bag. Carefully

machine stitch both the side panels into the "U" shape formed by the pencil case; do not be afraid to squash the bag a bit under the foot of the sewing machine in order to achieve this. Finish off by folding the bias binding over so that it hides the raw edges left after seaming. Pin, baste and neatly slipstitch, see page 96. Snip off any excess fabric at the end of the bias strips if necessary, but leave about 1.5cm (⅝in) to tuck in and finish off the corners with neat hand stitches.

12. Finally, slip a yellow wooden bead onto the end of each tie; make a knot to secure the bead and snip off any straggling threads.

ALTERNATIVE PROJECT

As an alternative to the pencil case, you can stitch this similar design (shown right) on a flat piece of waste canvas. Perhaps frame the embroidery as a picture, or make it into a cushion.

ABILITY LEVEL: *Intermediate*

MEASUREMENTS

The cross stitch design measures 17.5 x 8cm (7 x 3¼in)

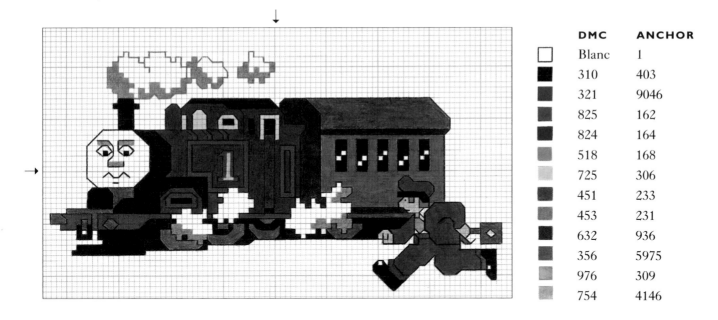

	DMC	ANCHOR
☐	Blanc	1
■	310	403
■	321	9046
■	825	162
■	824	164
■	518	168
■	725	306
■	451	233
■	453	231
■	632	936
■	356	5975
■	976	309
■	754	4146

MATERIALS

• Basic sewing kit (see page 92)
• One piece of 14-count waste canvas, 23 x 14cm (9¼ x 5⅝in), in white
• One piece of yellow fabric, 46 x 46cm (18⅜ x 18⅜in)
• A piece of interfacing, 23 x 14cm (9¼ x 5⅝in)
• Stranded cotton, one skein of each of the colours shown in the key (above right)
• Tapestry needle, size 24-26
• A 15cm (6in) embroidery hoop

TO EMBROIDER

Use two strands for the cross stitch, see page 95. Outline the train, the face, the man and the smoke in a single strand in backstitch, see page 95. Work the No 1 using two strands in backstitch. For the guard's eyes make French knots with one strand twisted twice around the needle, see page 97. Do not outline inside the smoke or inside the carriage windows where the highlights show.

TO MAKE UP

1. Centre the design on the piece of yellow fabric; measure carefully and use basting lines as a positional guide, see page 93. Pin and baste the piece of interfacing underneath and the piece of waste canvas on top of the yellow fabric to form a triple layer.

2. Fix the embroidery hoop around the middle of the area to be stitched and when all three layers of fabric, waste canvas and interfacing are good and taut start to cross stitch, see page 90.

3. Treat the finished embroidery as described on page 94.

Harold Drawstring Purse

As well as all sorts of trains, other vehicles come into several *Thomas the Tank Engine* stories, for instance the helicopter in *Percy and Harold*. "Percy worked hard at the harbour. Toby helped, but sometimes the loads of stone were too heavy, and Percy had to fetch them for himself. Then he would push the trucks along the quay to where the workmen needed the stone for their building. An airfield was close by, and Percy heard the aeroplanes

zooming overhead all day. The noisiest of all was a helicopter, which hovered, buzzing like an angry bee. 'Stupid thing!' said Percy, 'why can't it go and buzz somewhere else?' One day Percy stopped near the airfield. The helicopter was standing quite close. 'Hullo!' said Percy, 'who are you?' 'I'm Harold, who are you?' 'I'm Percy. What whirly great arms you've got.' 'They're nice arms,' said Harold, offended. 'I can hover like a bird. Don't you wish *you* could hover?' 'Certainly not; I like my rails, thank you.' 'I think railways are slow,' said Harold in a bored voice. 'They're not much use and quite out of date.' He whirled his arms and buzzed away. Percy found Toby at the top station arranging trucks. 'I say, Toby,' he burst out, 'that Harold, that stuck-up whirli-bird thing, says I'm slow and out of date. Just let him wait, I'll show him!' He collected his trucks and started off, still fuming. Soon, above the clatter of the trucks they heard a familiar buzzing. 'Percy,' whispered his driver, 'there's Harold. He's not far ahead. Let's race him.' 'Yes, let's,' said Percy excitedly."

From *Percy the Small Engine* by The Rev. W. Awdry

Harold the helicopter hovering above Percy (above); Harold stitched onto a handy drawstring purse (opposite).

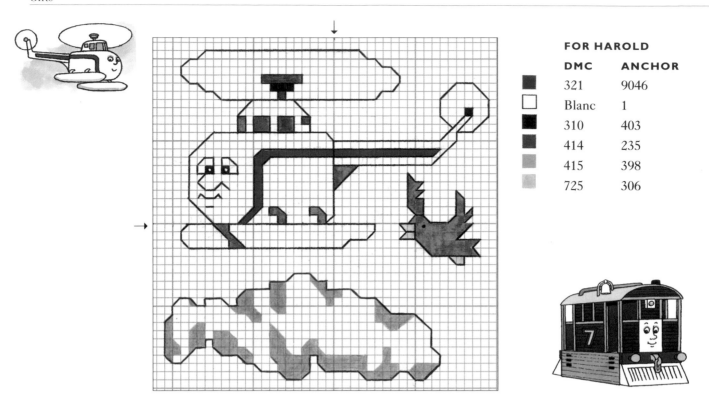

FOR HAROLD

	DMC	ANCHOR
■	321	9046
□	Blanc	1
■	310	403
■	414	235
■	415	398
■	725	306

ABILITY LEVEL: *Intermediate*

MEASUREMENTS

The cross stitch design measures 6.5 x 8cm
(2⅝ x 3¼in)

MATERIALS

• Basic sewing kit (see page 92)
• One piece of 14-count Aida, in red,
35.5 x 25cm (14¼ x 10in), in red
• Stranded cotton, one skein of each of the
colours shown in the key (above right)
• Tapestry needle, size 24-26
• A 15cm (6in) embroidery hoop
• Green cotton, one piece 33 x 23cm
(13¼ x 11¼in) and one strip 56 x 4cm
(22⅜ x 1⅝in)
• Red and green thread
• Four red wooden beads

TO EMBROIDER

Use three strands of thread for the main
cross stitch, see page 95. Work the face
of the helicopter and the propellors
with two strands of black in backstitch,
see page 95. For the cloud, backstitch
in one strand of dark gray. For the bird,
backstitch in one strand of black. Use a
single strand to make French knots to
highlight the eyes in white with two
twists around the needle, see page 97.
Use one strand for the bird's eye and
make a French knot with two twists
around the needle.

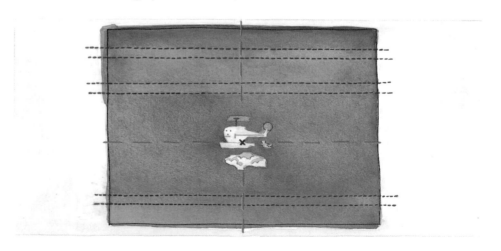

TO MAKE UP

1. Turn to page 102-103 and follow the pattern for this project. The basting line on page 103 indicates that the embroidery is not positioned exactly in the middle of the Aida; in fact the centre point of the embroidery is approximately 10cm (4in) from the bottom of the Aida. Use the basting line shown as a guide. Fix the hoop, complete the embroidery and treat when finished as described on page 94.

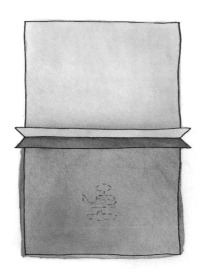

2. To make up the purse, trim down the embroidered piece of Aida so that it measures 33 x 23cm (13¼ x 11¼in). Cut a piece of green lining fabric to the same dimensions. With both pieces right sides together make a 1cm (⅜in) seam along the top edge of the purse.

3. Fold the joined fabrics in half lengthways and make another seam joining the two open edges; leave a 1.5cm (⅝in) hole

for the string to be drawn through (the position of the hole is marked by parallel dotted lines on the pattern on page 102 and on the diagram at the bottom of page 54).

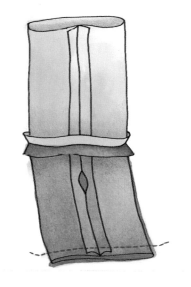

4. Sew along the bottom (the red Aida) end of the purse and leave the green lining end open. Turn the whole purse right side out.

5. Turn in the raw edges of the green lining and topstitch (see page 96) very close to the edge, or you can slipstitch (see page 96) instead. Push the lining down inside the purse. Press the open "mouth" of the purse with a cool iron so that the green lining lies neatly inside the purse and lies approximately 3mm (⅛in) below the "mouth".

6. Next mark two parallel lines with basting to form a "tunnel" for the drawstring, see the pair of parallel dotted

lines on the pattern on page 102 for guidance, and refer to the diagram at the bottom of page 54. The first line of basting falls 4cm (1⅝in) down from the mouth of the purse and a second line of basting 1.5cm (⅝in) below this; in this way the hole left previously falls between the two basting lines. Turn the purse wrong side out and machine stitch over both lines of basting to secure. Turn right side out again and snip away any loose threads.

7. To make the drawstring, cut a strip of green fabric 56 x 4cm (22⅜ x 1⅝in). Fold the strip in half lengthways, tuck in the raw edges, pin and baste so that the strip is approximately 1cm (⅜in) in width. Topstitch (see page 96) along the edge and press flat. Attach one end of the strip to a bodkin, or a safety pin, and push through the "tunnel". Gather the two ends of the strip to pull the purse shut and slip two red wooden beads on each end of the "string"; knot to secure and tie in a bow.

Fat Controller Book Mark

In *Thomas Comes to Breakfast* silly Thomas decides to leave his shed without his driver. He soon realizes his mistake as he runs out of control and eventually runs into the Fat Controller, who is not pleased. "Thomas's wheels left the rails and crunched the tarmac. 'Horrors!' he exclaimed, and shut his eyes. He didn't dare look at what was coming next. The station master's family were having breakfast. They were eating ham and eggs. There was a crash – the house rocked – broken glass tinkled – plaster peppered their plates. Thomas had collected a bush on his travels... 'You are a very naughty engine.' 'I know, Sir, I'm sorry, Sir.' Thomas's voice was muffled behind his bush. 'You must go to the Works, and have your front end mended. It will be a long job.' 'Yes, Sir,' faltered Thomas. 'Meanwhile,' said the Fat Controller, 'a Diesel Rail-car will do your work.' 'A D-D-Diesel, Sir?' Thomas spluttered. 'Yes, Thomas. Diesels *always* stay in their sheds till they are wanted...'"

From *Mountain Engines* by The Rev. W. Awdry

What better than to use a Fat Controller bookmark (above) when reading Thomas The Tank Engine stories.

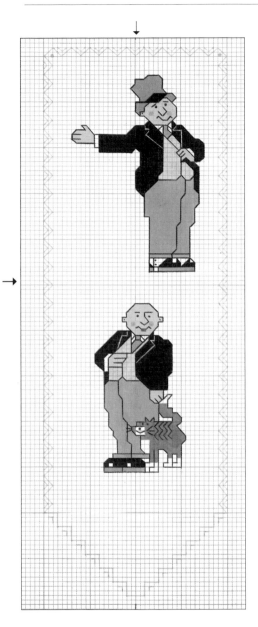

DMC	ANCHOR
415	398
976	309
758	868
760	9
725	306
Blanc	1
310	403

ABILITY LEVEL: *Easy*

MEASUREMENTS

The cross stitch design measures 6.5 x 18cm
(2⅝ x 7¼in)

MATERIALS

- Basic sewing kit (see page 92)
- One piece of 16-count Aida, 22.5 x 22.5cm
  (9 x 9in), in gray
- Stranded cotton, one skein of each of the
  colours shown in the key (below left)
- Tapestry needle, size 24-26
- A 15cm (6in) embroidery hoop
- One piece of batting, 7.5 x 20cm (3 x 8in)
- One piece of white felt, 7.5 x 20cm (3 x 8in)
- One piece of stiffening, 7.5 x20cm (3 x 8in)

TO EMBROIDER

Use a single strand for the cross stitch,
see page 95. Outline the motifs using a
single strand of black in backstitch, see
page 95. Backstitch the lapels of the Fat
Controller's jacket in a single strand of
white. For the ears and spats make
French knots with a single strand and
one twist around the needle, see page
97. For the eyes make French knots
with two twists around the needle. For
the edging, use two strands working in
long stitch, see page 96.

Centre the design on the Aida; measure carefully and use basting lines as a
positional guide, see page 93. Fix the
embroidery hoop in the middle of the
area to be stitched and start to cross
stitch. Treat the finished embroidery
as described on page 94.

TO MAKE UP

1. Cut out one piece of batting, one of
felt and one of stiffening, following the
pattern shown on page 103. Then cut
out the embroidered piece of Aida
to the same pattern plus a 1.5cm (⅝in)
seam allowance all round.

2. Place the stiffening and the batting
on the wrong side of the embroidered
piece of Aida, positioned centrally.
Fold down the raw edge of the Aida
over the batting, pin and baste down.

3. Place the piece of felt over the
reverse side of the bookmark, to overlap the basting in the previous step.
Oversew by hand around
the edge (see page 96).

4. To finish, make a
tassle from a piece of
yellow DMC (no 725).
Cut the yarn about 5cm
(2in) long and hand sew
it to the point of the
bookmark.

Snowdrift Christmas Card

This Christmas card shows a wintry scene from the story *Thomas, Terence and the Snow*. "'You'll need your snow plough for the next journey, Thomas,' said the driver. 'Pooh! Snow is silly soft stuff – it won't stop me.' 'Listen to me,' his driver replied, 'we are going to fix your snow plough on, and I want no nonsense, please.' The snow plough was heavy and uncomfortable and made Thomas cross. He shook it, and he banged it and when they got back it was so damaged that the driver had to take it off. 'You're a very naughty engine,' said his driver, as he shut the shed door that night. Next morning, both driver and fireman came early and worked hard to mend the snow plough; but they couldn't make it fit properly. It was time for the first train. Thomas was pleased, 'I shan't have to wear it...' he puffed to Annie and Clarabel. 'I hope it's alright...' they whispered anxiously to each other.

The driver was anxious, too '...it's sure to be deep in the valley.' It was snowing again when Thomas started, but the rails were not covered. 'Silly soft stuff!...' he puffed. 'I didn't need that stupid old thing yesterday; I shan't today. Snow can't stop me,' and he rushed into the tunnel, thinking how clever he was. At the other end he saw a heap of snow fallen from the sides of the cutting. 'Silly old snow,' said Thomas, and charged it. 'Cinders and ashes!' said Thomas, 'I'm stuck!' – and he was!"

From *Tank Engine Thomas Again* by The Rev. W. Awdry

For a very special Christmas card you can recreate this festive scene of Thomas in the snow in stitching. As with the birthday card on page 60, the card frame protects the design so it can be kept and enjoyed as a miniature picture.

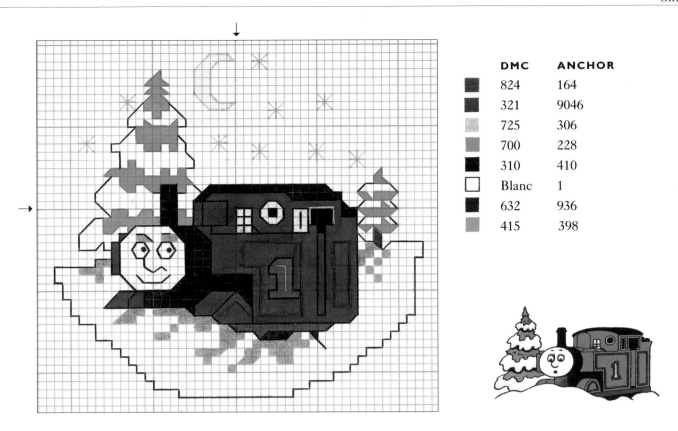

DMC	ANCHOR
824	164
321	9046
725	306
700	228
310	410
Blanc	1
632	936
415	398

ABILITY LEVEL: *Easy*

MEASUREMENTS

The finished card measures 11 x 15.5cm (4¼ x 6in) and the circumference of the circular cut-away is 8cm (3in)

MATERIALS

• Basic sewing kit (see page 92)
• One piece of 14-count Aida, 23 x 23cm (9 x 9in), in dusty blue
• A 15cm (6in) embroidery hoop
• Stranded cotton, one skein of each of the colours shown in the key (above right)
• Tapestry needle, size 24-26
• One Anchor gift card with a circular cut-away (available from a good haberdasher and includes a self-adhesive mount board)

TO EMBROIDER

Use three strands for the cross stitch, see page 95. Outline the moon in one strand of yellow in backstitch, see page 95. Outline the trees in backstitch in a single strand of white and green. Backstitch the face in two black strands. For the eyes use two strands, making French knots by twisting the thread twice around the needle, see page 97. Stitch the stars in backstitch with two strands. The No. 1 and windows are backstitched in two strands. The red markings on the train are backstitched in two strands, the snow outline is backstitched in one strand. The other details on the train are outlined in backstitch in one strand.

TO MAKE UP

1. First centre the design on the Aida; to do this make careful measurements and use basting lines as a positional guide, see page 93.

2. Fix the embroidery hoop and start stitching. Note that the limit of the snowy background should just overlap the edge of the circular cut-away so no Aida is left visible.

3. Treat the finished embroidery as described on page 94.

4. Follow the instructions included in the purchased card kit to complete the making-up process.

59

Happy Birthday Card

This card design is taken from the story *Coal*. "The Fat Controller was waiting when Henry came to the platform. He had taken off his hat and coat, and put on overalls. He climbed to the footplate and Henry started. 'Henry is a "bad steamer",' said the fireman. 'I build up his fire, but it doesn't give enough heat.' Henry tried very hard, but it was no good. He had not enough steam, and they stopped outside Edward's station. 'Oh dear!' thought Henry sadly, 'I shall have to go away.' Edward took charge of the train. Henry stopped behind. 'What do you think is wrong, fireman?' asked the Fat Controller. The fireman mopped his face. 'Excuse me, Sir,' he answered, 'but the coal is wrong. We've had a poor lot lately, and today it's worse. The other engines can manage; they have big fireboxes. Henry's is small and can't make the heat. With Welsh coal he'd be a different engine.' 'It's expensive,' said the Fat Controller thoughtfully, 'but Henry must have a fair chance. James shall go and fetch some.' When the Welsh coal came, Henry's driver and fireman were excited. 'Now we'll show them...'"

From *Henry the Green Engine* by The Rev. W. Awdry

Smiling Henry has an engine full of new coal on this birthday card. After stitching, keep the card in its mount for display.

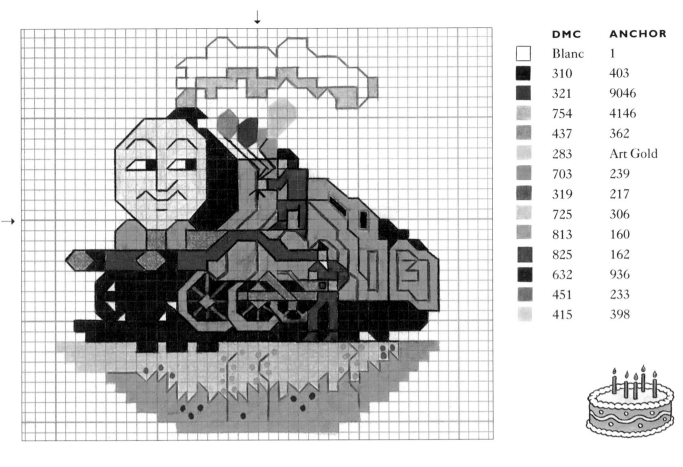

	DMC	ANCHOR
☐	Blanc	1
■	310	403
■	321	9046
▨	754	4146
▨	437	362
▨	283	Art Gold
▨	703	239
▨	319	217
▨	725	306
▨	813	160
■	825	162
■	632	936
▨	451	233
▨	415	398

ABILITY LEVEL: *Easy*

MEASUREMENTS

The cross stitch design measures 7.5 x 7cm
(3 x 2¾in)

MATERIALS

- Basic sewing kit (see page 92)
- One piece of 14-count Aida, 18 x 8cm (7¼ x 3¼in), in white
- Stranded cotton, one skein of each of the colours shown in the key (above right)
- Tapestry needle, size 24-26
- A 15cm (6in) embroidery hoop
- One Anchor gift card (from a good haberdasher, with self-adhesive mount)

TO EMBROIDER

Use two strands to work the cross stitch, see page 95. For the flowers make French knots by twisting two strands twice around the needle, see page 97. Work the No 3 and the train's face using two strands, working in backstitch, see page 95. Outline the balloons, the clouds, the train, and stitch the flower stems all using a single strand.

TO MAKE UP

1. Fold the piece of Aida in half widthways and lengthways to find the centre point. Mark the fold lines with contrasting basting thread. Centre the design on the Aida, using the basting lines as a positional guide, see page 93.

2. Fix the hoop in the middle of the area to be stitched and start to cross stitch in the middle of the piece of Aida.

3. To treat the finished embroidery, see page 94.

4. Follow the manufacturer's instructions to mount the birthday card.

Whistle Key Ring

This useful key ring shows the guard on one side and his whistle on the other. In the extract from this story, *Tenders for Henry*, the whistle blows to signal a train out of the station. "'I'm not happy,' complained Gordon. 'Your fire-box is out of order,' said James. 'No wonder, after all that coal you had yesterday.' 'Hard work brings good appetite,' snapped Gordon. '*You* wouldn't understand.' 'I know,' put in Duck, brightly. 'It's boiler-ache. I warned you about that standpipe on the other railway; but you drank gallons.' ...Gordon backed down on his train, hissing mournfully. 'Cheer up, Gordon!' said the Fat Controller. 'I can't, Sir. The others say I've got boiler-ache, but I haven't, Sir. Is it true, Sir, what the diesels, say?' 'What do they say?' 'They boast that they've abolished Steam, Sir.' 'Yes, Gordon. It is true.' 'What, Sir! All my Doncaster brothers, drawn the same time as me?' 'All gone, except one.' The guard's whistle blew, and Gordon puffed sadly away. 'Poor old Gordon!' said the Fat Controller. 'Hmm...If only we could!...Yes, I'll ask his owner at once.' He hurried away. Arrangements took time, but one evening, Gordon's driver ran back, excited. 'Wake up, Gordon! The Fat Controller's given you a surprise. Look!' Gordon could hardly believe it. Backing towards him were two massive green tenders, and their engine's shape was very like his own. 'It's Flying Scotsman!' he gasped."

From *Enterprising Engines* by The Rev. W. Awdry

Why not buy a transparent plastic key ring like the one shown above left and liven it up with a guard and whistle in cross stitch.

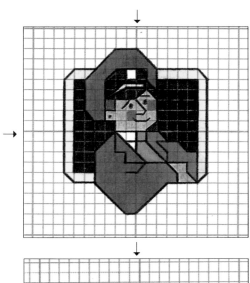

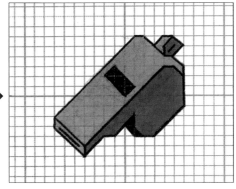

FOR THE GUARD

	DMC	ANCHOR
■	825	162
▨	725	306
▨	415	398
□	Blanc	1
■	310	403
▨	754	4146
▨	760	9
▨	3776	349

FOR THE WHISTLE

	DMC	ANCHOR
■	310	403
▨	415	398
■	414	235

ABILITY LEVEL: *Easy*

MEASUREMENTS

The finished key ring measures 3cm (1¼in) in diameter

MATERIALS

- Basic sewing kit (see page 92)
- One piece of 14-count Aida, 15 x 27cm (5¾ x 10¾in), in white (this is enough to work both designs)
- A 10cm (4in) embroidery hoop
- Stranded cotton, one skein of each of the colours shown in the keys (below left)
- Tapestry needle, size 24-26
- One round, transparent plastic key ring
- One small piece of interfacing, just bigger than the size of the key ring
- A pencil or fabric marker
- Fabric glue

TO EMBROIDER

For the guard and the whistle, cross stitch using two strands separated off from the main skein, see page 95. For the whistle, use a single strand of black from the main skein for the outline and work in backstitch, see page 95. Backstitch the ends of the whistle working with two strands of thread. For the guard, backstitch with a single strand to make the black outline. For the eyes use one strand of black and make a French knot by twisting the thread twice around the needle, see page 97. For the ear on the guard, make a French knot in the same way but this time twisting only once around the needle.

TO MAKE UP

1. First centre the two designs on the Aida; measure carefully and use basting lines as a positional guide, see page 93.

2. Fix the hoop and start stitching.

3. Treat the finished embroidery as described on page 94.

4. Measure the size of the inside of the key ring; transfer the measurements to a piece of interfacing and mark a circular outline with a pencil or fabric marker; cut out just inside the marked outline.

5. Cut out the two finished designs so both have exactly the same diameter and circumference as the circle of interfacing; be careful not to fray the edges.

6. Place the circle of interfacing between the two circular designs and with a small dab of glue secure the layers together.

7. Insert into the key ring so there is an image on both sides.

Gordon Cake Band

Although Gordon is a high-speed engine, in the story *Fire Escape* he has a problem with his fire and doesn't run as fast as usual. "They were halfway up the hill when there was a clatter beneath Gordon's cab. Suddenly he felt a blast of cold air in his middle, as if there were a gap between his boiler and cab. 'Ooooof!' he gasped. 'What's happened?' The fireman looked at his fire: there was a gaping hole in the middle, where the firebars had collapsed and a large part of the fire had disappeared. 'You've lost part of your fire, Gordon,' the fireman explained. 'What a place to do it!' Already Gordon was feeling

weaker. Without a full fire his steam pressure and speed fell quickly. But his driver knew what to do. 'Find the biggest piece of coal you can, and put it across the hole,' he told the fireman. 'That will stop some of the cold air from getting in, and we'll be able to hold steam better. But hurry, or the hill will beat us!' The fireman hurried. A large lump of coal lay near the front of the tender. Quickly he moved it into place with his shovel and a long steel bar. Gordon felt better at once."

From *Gordon the Highspeed Engine* by The Rev. W. Awdry

This cake band will make a birthday, or any other celebration, cake all the more special and it can be used again and again.

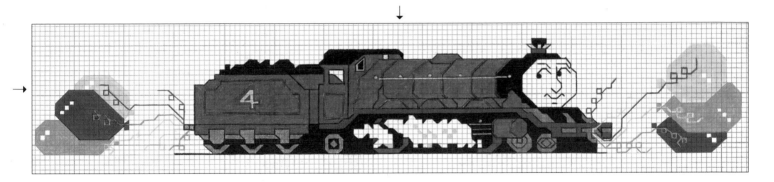

	DMC	ANCHOR
■	451	233
■	321	9046
▨	743	305
■	310	403
▨	825	162
▨	415	398
□	Blanc	1
■	518	168

ABILITY LEVEL: *Easy*

MEASUREMENTS

The cross stitch design measures 24 x 3.5cm (9⅝x 1⅜in)

MATERIALS

• Basic sewing kit (see page 92)
• One band of 14-count Aida, in white (cut to a length 16cm (6⅜in) longer than the circumference of the cake)
• Piece of calico or cotton, the square of the length of the Aida band measured above
• Stranded cotton, one skein of each of the colours shown in the key (above)
• Tapestry needle, size 24-26
• A 15cm (6in) embroidery hoop
• Strip of touch-and-close fastening 4cm (1⅜in) long

TO EMBROIDER

Use two strands for the cross stitch, see page 95. Use two strands to work all the red markings and the number 4 on the train in backstitch, see page 95. For the coloured ribbons use two strands in backstitch. Outline the train in black with a single strand in backstitch. For the yellow strip across the body of the train and the face work in two strands in backstitch. Work the eyes in French knots with two strands, making two twists around the needle, see page 97. Work the yellow French knots in the same way. For the gray pipes round the smoke use two strands in backstitch and make a French knot with two twists around the needle.

TO MAKE UP

1. Baste the edges of the measured cake band onto two pieces of calico to stabilize it for stitching. Centre the design on the Aida; measure carefully and use basting lines as a positional guide, see page 93. Fix the embroidery hoop in the middle of the area to be stitched and start to cross stitch. When finished, remove the calico or cotton backing.

Treat the finished embroidery as described on page 94.

2. The embroidered band of Aida should be 16cm (6⅜in) longer than the circumference of the cake in order to allow for an overlap. Turn back 6cm (2⅜in) at one end of the Aida band and fold in another 0.5cm (¼in) to hide the raw edge. Pin and baste down with wrong sides together, making a neat rectangle of stitches. Repeat for the opposite end of the Aida band.

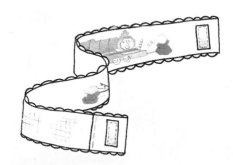

3. Take the 4cm (1⅜in) long strip of touch-and-close and oversew one side of the strip to either end of the Aida band on the inside (wrong side) of the turned-under edges, to fasten. The cake band should fit comfortably around the cake.

Soft Furnishings

Opposite Like many of the other projects in the book, this cushion is made from hard-wearing cotton in bold, primary colours that will delight children and are fun to sew with; it goes well with the lampshade.
Below The design on the cushion shown opposite was inspired by this original illustration from the story *Henry and the Elephant*. To make this cushion yourself, turn to page 74.

All of the projects in this chapter require some sewing know-how. The curtain project shows you how to trim a swathe of cotton with a decorative cross stitch border, so you can transform a pair of ordinary, plain drapes into something much more stylish and colourful. And the matching tie-back provides an extra flourish to give the whole window dressing a professional look. The cushion project would make a lovely addition to a child's room, or a perfect gift. The lampshade is in fact quite simple to make: once you have completed the cross stitch design, cut out and attach the embroidered fabric to correspond to the dimensions of a ready-made shade. When switched on, the light throws the design into silhouette. The charming lampshade makes bed-time reading all the more enjoyable. The toy bag is made from the same cheerful cotton as the cushion, so the two would complement each other well in a child's bedroom or a playroom.

Cows! Curtains

In the story *Cows!* Edward comes across a herd of cows on the railway line, and this led to my curtain design. "Edward the blue engine was getting old. His bearings were worn, and he clanked as he puffed along. He was taking twenty empty cattle trucks to a market-town. The sun shone, the birds sang, and some cows grazed in a field by the line. 'Come on! come on! come on!' puffed Edward. 'Oh! oh! oh!' screamed the trucks. Edward puffed and clanked; the trucks rattled and screamed. The cows were not used to trains; the noise and smoke disturbed them. They twitched up their tails and ran. They galloped across the field, broke through the fence, and charged the train between the thirteenth and fourteenth trucks. The coupling broke, and the last seven trucks left the rails. They were not damaged, and stayed upright. They ran for a short way along the sleepers before stopping. Edward felt a jerk but didn't take much notice. He was used to trucks. 'Bother those trucks!' he thought. 'Why can't they come quietly?' He ran

on to the next station before either he or his driver realised what had happened. When Gordon and Henry heard about the accident, they laughed and laughed. 'Fancy allowing cows to break his train! They wouldn't dare do that to US. WE'd show them!' they boasted... 'You couldn't help it, Edward,' he said. 'They've never met cows. I have, and I know the trouble they are.'"

From *Edward the Blue Engine* by The Rev. W. Awdry

Edward casts a worried glance at some playful cows (above). You can liven up a pair of plain curtains by embellishing them with a cross-stitched border inspired by the story Cows! To make the window dressing all the more attractive, sew a matching tie-back (opposite).

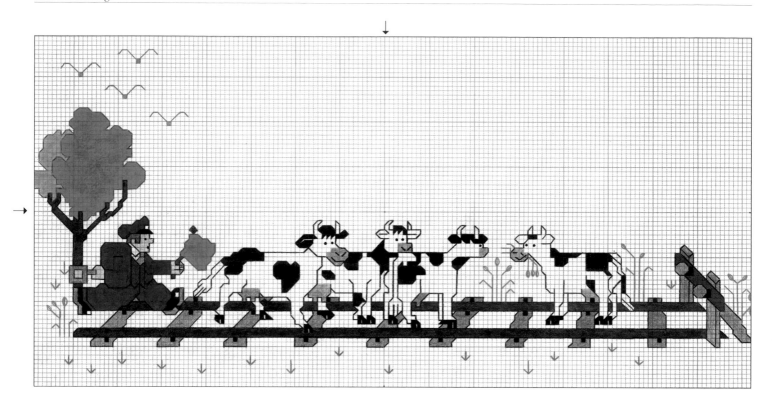

FOR THE CURTAIN

	DMC	ANCHOR
☐	Blanc	1
■	310	403
	754	4146
	321	9046
	3776	349
	451	233
	725	306
	703	239
	700	228
	890	683
	825	162
	632	936
	415	398

ABILITY LEVEL: *Intermediate*

MEASUREMENTS

The cross stitch design measures 13 x 28cm (5¼ x 11¼in)

MATERIALS

For the curtain

- Basic sewing kit (see page 92)
- One piece of 14-count waste canvas, 35 x 17.5cm (14 x 7in)
- A piece of interfacing, 35 x 17.5cm (14 x 7in)
- Yellow cotton, 112cm (45in) width and long enough for the height of your window
- White cotton lining, the same measurements as the above yellow cotton
- Stranded cotton, one skein of each of the colours shown in the key (left)
- Tapestry needle, size 24-26
- A 15cm (6in) embroidery hoop
- Cotton thread to match the yellow fabric

For the tie-back

- Basic sewing kit (see page 92)
- One piece of 14-count waste canvas, 18 x 22.5cm (7¼ x 9in)
- One piece of interfacing, 18 x 22.5cm (7¼ x 9in)
- A 15cm (6in) embroidery hoop
- One piece of batting, 18 x 22.5cm (7¼ x 9in)
- Seven lengths of red fabric for bias binding; one 52.5 x 3.5cm (21 x 1⅜in); one 55 x 3.5cm (22 x 1⅜in); three 42.5 x 3.5cm (17 x 1⅜in) and two 3 x 7.5cm (1¼ x 3in)
- Cotton thread to match the red fabric
- Yellow cotton, 40 x 55cm (16 x 22in)

TO EMBROIDER THE CURTAIN

Use two strands for the cross stitch, see page 95. Embroider the grass with two strands in backstitch, see page 95.

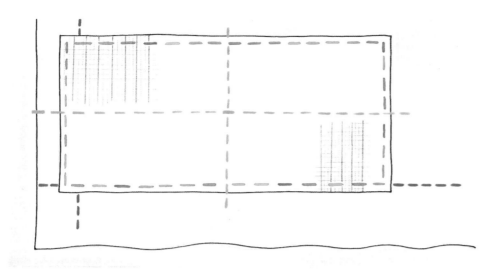

place with pins, and position the waste canvas on top of the yellow fabric so that it overlaps the interfacing. For instructions on how to use waste canvas and interfacing, see page 90. Baste all around the edge of the waste canvas through all three layers of fabric. Fix the hoop over the middle of the design and work outwards, moving the hoop as you progress. Treat the finished embroidery as described on page 94. Repeat for the left-hand curtain but work in a mirror image so that both curtains match.

For the grassheads use two strands working in chain stitch, see page 97. For the birds' wings backstitch using two strands. Outline the trees with a single strand in backstitch. To make the guard's eyes and mouth and the cows' eyes use two strands to make French knots by twisting the yarn twice around the needle, see page 97.

TO MAKE THE CURTAIN

1. To position the embroidery on the yellow fabric start with the right-hand curtain. Lay the piece of yellow cotton out flat and pin and baste a horizontal line 12.5cm (5in) above the bottom raw edge. Pin and baste a vertical line 6cm (2⅜in) in from the outside selvedge. This marks the outer limit of the embroidery and allows for a 2.5cm (1in) turn on the selvedge and a 6cm (2⅜in) hem along the bottom of the curtain. A border of yellow fabric runs between the embroidery and the edge of the curtain.

2. Mark a vertical and a horizontal line of basting stitches onto the yellow cotton as a positional guide for the embroidery, see page 93 for how to position a design and also refer to the illustration above. Place the piece of interfacing under the yellow cotton, so that it covers the embroidery area. Hold the interfacing in

3. Once the embroidery is complete and treated leave it to air for a day or so before you sew up the curtain. Repeat the process for the second curtain. To make the curtain you should refer to a soft furnishing book and follow guidelines for measuring up a window and making a pair of lined curtains.

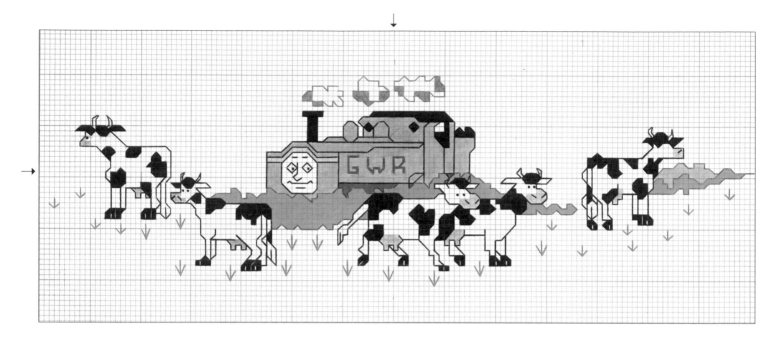

FOR THE TIE-BACK

	DMC	ANCHOR
	703	239
	700	228
	319	217
	725	306
	453	231
	758	868
	321	9046
	Blanc	1
	310	403

TO EMBROIDER THE TIE-BACK

Use two strands for the cross stitch. Outline the trains, cows and bushes in a single strand of black in backstitch. Outline the letters on the train in backstitch with three strands. Outline the smoke in a single strand. Backstitch the face with two strands. Use a single strand for the cows' eyes making French knots by twisting the yarn twice around the needle. Work the holes of the cows' noses and the grass tufts using two strands in longstitch, see page 96.

TO MAKE THE TIE-BACK

1. Cut out a piece of yellow fabric large enough to trace the pattern of the tie-back shown on page 107, leaving an allowance to fix to an embroidery hoop; 40 x 55cm (16 x 22in) is sufficient. Trace off the pattern with a fabric marker. Place a piece of interfacing under and a piece of waste canvas on top of the fabric. Centre the design; measure carefully and use basting lines as a positional guide for all three layers, see page 93. Fix the hoop and start stitching. To treat the finished embroidery, see page 94.

2. Cut out the embroidered pattern to the dimensions shown on page 107. Cut out a piece of backing in the same yellow fabric.

Cut out some batting, or else use a piece of stiff fabric in order to give the tie-back some body and weight. Sandwich the batting or the stiffening between the two yellow pieces of fabric. Then pin and baste the layers together just inside the 1.2cm (½in) seam allowance.

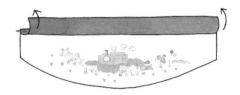

3. Cut the bias binding to the required lengths. Take the strip that is 52.5 x 3.5cm (21 x 1⅜in) long and pin and baste it along the straight edge of the right side of the tie-back. Machine sew in place. Fold over the binding strip, tuck under, pin, baste and then oversew by hand

(see page 96). Repeat to trim the curved edge of the tie-back using the strip of bias binding that is 55 x 3.5cm (22 x 1⅜in) long. Leave each end of the tie-back with a raw edge for now.

4. To make the loops that will hold the tie-back in place, take the three strips of bias binding that each measure 42.5 x 3.5cm (17 x 1⅜in) long. For each strip, tuck under the long raw edges, pin, baste and sew so that they form a "rouleau" strip. Baste one end of each strip together and hold all three ends together with a safety pin. Attach the pin to something firm like a piece of upholstery. Plait the three strips and secure the end with basting or a few machine stitches.

5. Cut the finished plait into two 11cm (4⅜in) lengths and machine sew the ends back and forth a couple of times to secure; these form the loops. Attach the loops to each short end of the tie-back on the embroidered side.

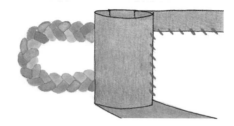

6. Pin and baste the prepared piece of bias binding that is 3cm (1¼in) wide and 7.5cm (3in) long to trim each short end of the tie-back. Fold over the raw edges,

and sew them in place by machine. Then turn over the binding strip and hand sew to finish on the wrong side of the tie-back. Repeat steps 1 to 5 to make the second tie-back. Fix a hook to the wall just outside the window frame at the desired height. Hang one loop on the hook, work it around the hanging curtain so that the design is the correct way up and fix the second loop onto the hook. Do exactly the same for the opposite curtain, making sure the hooks are fixed at an equal level; this completes the window treatment.

Henry and the Elephant Cushion

The design on this cushion cover is inspired by *Henry and the Elephant.* "One morning Henry was told to take some workmen to a tunnel which was blocked... The workmen took their tools and went inside. Suddenly with a shout they all ran out looking frightened. 'We went to the block and started to dig, but it grunted and moved,' they said. 'Rubbish,' said the foreman. 'It's not rubbish, it's big and alive; we're not going in there again.' 'Right,' said the foreman. 'I'll ride in a truck and Henry shall push it out.' 'Wheeesh,' said Henry unhappily. He

hated tunnels (he had been shut up in one once), but this was worse, something big and alive was inside. 'Peep peep peep pip pip pee–eep!' he whistled, 'I don't want to go in!' 'Neither do I,' said his driver, 'but we must clear the line.' 'Oh dear! Oh dear!' puffed Henry as they slowly advanced into the darkness. BUMP —!!!! Henry's driver shut off steam at once. 'Help! Help! we're going back,' wailed Henry, and slowly moving out into the day-

light came first Henry, then the trucks, and last of all, pushing hard and rather cross, came a large elephant. 'Well I never did!' said the foreman. 'It's an elephant from the Circus.' ...They gave him some sandwiches and cake, so he forgot he was cross and remembered he was hungry. He drank three buckets of water without stopping, and was just going to drink another when Henry let off steam. The elephant jumped, and 'hoo——oosh', he squirted the water over Henry by mistake. Poor Henry!"

From *Troublesome Engines* by The Rev. W. Awdry

In the story Henry and the Elephant a circus is transported on the railway line (above). This brightly coloured cushion echoes a scene from the story and is designed to complement the other soft furnishing projects featured in this chapter (opposite).

	DMC	ANCHOR
☐	Blanc	1
■	310	403
■	825	162
▨	704	238
▨	743	279
▨	754	4146
■	321	9046
▨	451	233
▨	415	398

ABILITY LEVEL: *Advanced*

MEASUREMENTS

The cross stitch design measures 17 x 16cm (6¾ x 6⅜in); the finished cushion measures 38 x 38cm (15¼ x 15¼in)

MATERIALS

• Basic sewing kit (see page 92)
• One piece of 14-count waste canvas, 19 x 19cm (7⅝ x 7⅝in)
• A piece of interfacing, 19 x 19cm (7⅝ x 7⅝in)
• Stranded cotton, one skein of each of the colours shown in the key (above)
• Tapestry needle, size 24-26
• A 15cm (6in) embroidery hoop
• One piece of yellow cotton, 112 x 50cm (45 x 20in)
• A piece of red cotton, 112 x 50cm (45 x 20in)
• Red and yellow thread to match
• One cushion, 38 x 38cm (15¼ x 15¼in)

TO EMBROIDER

Use two strands to work the cross stitch, see page 95. Work the water spout, the face of the train and the bucket handles in two strands working in backstitch, see

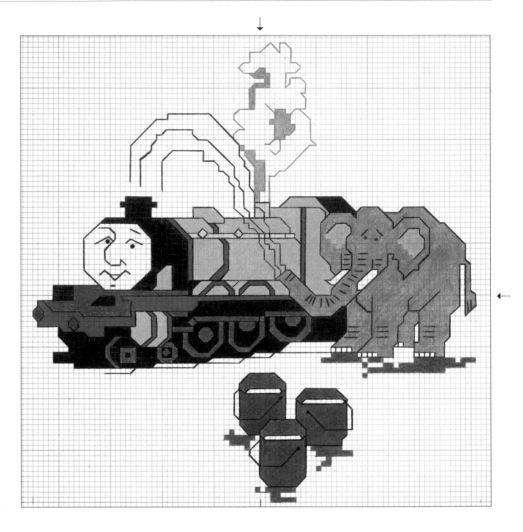

page 95. Outline all other parts of the design in a single strand in backstitch. For the eyes and the bucket handle joints make French knots with two strands twisting twice around the needle, see page 97.

TO MAKE UP

1. Centre the design on a square of yellow cotton slightly larger all round than pattern B on page 109, to allow for fixing the hoop. Position the piece of waste canvas (see page 90) centrally on top of

the square of yellow cotton and position the piece of interfacing centrally underneath the yellow fabric. Centre the design on all three layers; measure carefully and use basting lines as a guide, see page 93. Fix the hoop in the middle of the area to be embroidered and start to stitch. Treat the finished embroidery as described on page 94. Cut out the piece of yellow embroidered fabric according to pattern B on page 109. Press in the raw edges by 1cm (⅜in) ready to appliqué onto the front of the cushion.

2. Refer to the four patterns shown on pages 108-109. Cut out pattern A in red cotton; this is the back of the cushion. Cut out pattern C four times in red cotton; these form a frame on the front of the cushion. Cut out pattern D four times in yellow cotton; these form the edges of the cushion. The measurements on the pattern pieces include an all-round 1cm (⅜in) seam allowance.

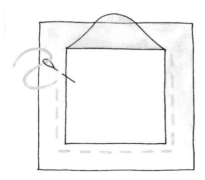

3. Turn under and press the seam allowance on both short, angled edges of *two* of the strips cut from pattern C. Lay them over the other two strips cut from the same pattern (with no seam allowance turn). Carefully match the angles and neatly top stitch at all four corners (see page 96).

4. Lay the embroidered piece of yellow cotton with the right side facing inside the red cotton border that you have just sewn in the previous step. Pin, baste and neatly topstitch the edges of the embroidered appliqué panel to the inside edges of the red border. This forms the front of the cushion cover.

5. To make the edging for the cushion, sew the pointed edges of all four pieces of yellow cotton wrong sides together by machine; keep the points exact. Trim the points with the scissors to about 0.25cm (⅛in). Turn right side out and poke out the points with the point of the scissors. Fold the strips of yellow cotton in half lengthways, as indicated on pattern D to form a border. Press flat, pin and baste the inside raw edges.

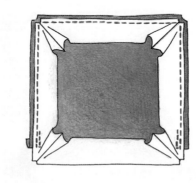

6. Turn the outer yellow border made in the previous step wrong side out once again. Take the back panel of red cotton (pattern A) and pin and baste around three sides of the outer edge of the yellow border to three sides of the outer edge of pattern A. Machine stitch around three sides of the cushion. Oversew by machine to strengthen about 2.5cm (1in) above each open edge. Fold down the fourth (open) edge of the red backing panel. Press and pin the open edge of the red backing panel out of the way before attaching the front panel to the border.

7. Press the raw edges of the yellow embroidered panel inwards. Position centrally over the back panel and border, wrong sides together. Pin, baste and machine sew together; align the corners. Overlap the red border 0.25cm (⅛in) over the yellow outer border and machine stitch with red thread on red fabric. Turn over the cushion and machine stitch with yellow thread on yellow fabric on the reverse side so that no stitches appear on the underside of the cushion; only on the border.

8. Finally, insert the cushion and neatly oversew the open edge (see page 96).

Green Flag Lampshade

On this lampshade you can see the Fat Controller and the guard waving his flag. For a Fat Controller story turn to page 56. Here is an extract from the story *Stop Thief!* which features Thomas, the guard and his flag. "Thomas stood at Ffarquhar, the top station of his branch line. He had run round Annie and Clarabel after the morning journey and was enjoying a short rest before the run back down the valley. His driver and fireman stood beside his cab, talking to the guard who had brought startling news. 'Did you know that the stationmaster was burgled last night?' he was asking. Thomas's driver shook his head. 'You don't say!' he exclaimed. 'I didn't know he had anything worth stealing.' 'He's won cups for gardening,' explained the fireman. 'All taken, and then the scoundrels had the cheek to pinch his car to carry them away in!' 'Not that new one he's so proud of?' said the driver. The guard nodded, and at that moment the signal rose to show that the line was clear. The driver and fireman climbed into Thomas's cab, the guard blew his whistle, waved his green flag and got into Clarabel, and Thomas set off. By the time they were through the tunnel the train was running nicely. Road and railway were beside each other here, with only a stream between them. Thomas remembered his race with Bertie the bus: he had only won because he could go through the hill, while Bertie had to go over it (see page 36). A flash of colour on the road ahead caught his eye. He tried to go faster to look more closely. 'Steady, Thomas,' said his driver. 'There's plenty of time.' 'Can't we get closer to that car,' panted Thomas. 'It looks like the station master's to me.'"

From *Really Useful Engines* by The Rev. W. Awdry

At the wave of a green flag Thomas, Clarabel and the guard set off in pursuit of what turns out to be the station master's stolen car (above).
Turn an ordinary lampshade into something special by decorating it with characters from the railway (opposite).

DMC	ANCHOR
754	4146
725	306
703	239
321	9046
760	9
310	403
Blanc	1
453	231
451	233
976	309
632	936
825	162

ABILITY LEVEL: *Easy*

MEASUREMENTS

The cross stitch design measures 45 x11.5cm
(18 x 4⅝in)

MATERIALS

- Basic sewing kit (see page 92)
- A piece of interfacing, 40 x 40cm (16 x 16in)
- One piece of 14-count waste canvas, 40 x 40cm (16 x 16in)
- A 15cm (6in) embroidery hoop
- Stranded cotton, one skein of each of the colours shown in the key (above)
- Tapestry needle, size 24-26
- A pair of tweezers
- One piece of yellow cotton 61 x 41cm (24⅜ x 16⅜in)
- Yellow thread to match above
- Light-coloured bedside lampshade
- Masking tape
- Two strips of bias binding, 2.5cm (1in) wide in red: 37.5cm (15in) and 75cm (30in) long
- Strong fabric glue

A: 34.5cm (13¾in)

B: 72.5cm (29in)

C: 16.5cm (6⅝in)

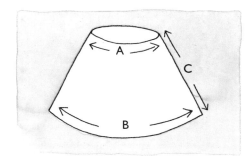

TO EMBROIDER

Use a single strand of black separated off from the main skein to make an outline around all the embroidery, to do this work in backstitch, see page 95. For the eyes and the buttons on the figures, make French knots using one strand of thread twisted once around the needle, see page 97.

TO MAKE UP

1. Place the lampshade pattern, shown on pages 106-107, in the middle of the piece of yellow cotton. Position the embroidery design on the yellow cotton and mark the centre point of the design with a vertical and a horizontal line of basting line, see page 93. Place the piece of interfacing under the yellow fabric and the waste canvas on top. Baste all three layers together. Stretch the hoop over the central part of the canvas and start to embroider working from the middle outwards and stitching through all three layers. Treat the embroidery as described on page 94.

2. To make up the lampshade, trace and cut out the pattern on pages 106-107 on the already embroidered yellow fabric. Wrap the embroidered fabric around

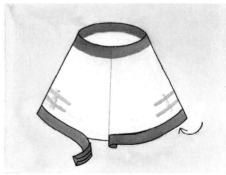

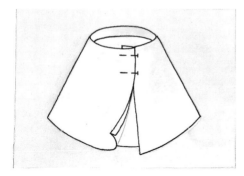

3. Trim the seam allowances around the top and bottom of the fabric lampshade to approximately 1cm (⅜in). Glue around the inside of the top and bottom rim of

and carefully press the shorter strip of binding around the top rim, beginning at the seam. Do not use too much glue or it will show through the fabric and ruin the overall look. The binding should stand approximately 0.5cm (¼in) above the top rim; then fold it over and glue all round to the inside of the shade to form a neat finish. The bias binding is not only a decorative trim but it also hides any raw edges of the yellow fabric. Repeat to finish the bottom rim of the lampshade using the longer strip of bias binding. Allow the whole to dry out thoroughly before use.

the purchased lampshade, carefully aligning the seams. Use masking tape to help with accurate alignment if preferred. Where the two straight sides meet turn under the raw edge and pin in position while the fabric is still on the lampshade base. Remove the fabric from the lampshade base, and baste and join either with topstitch or slipstitch, see page 96. Replace over the lampshade base to ensure the seams align and that the fit is good.

the lampshade base and turn over the raw edges of the fabric shade; press down firmly to stick.

4. Next add the bias binding. Apply a small amount of glue around the outside top rim of the fabric-covered lampshade

Henry Toy Bag

The design on this toy bag shows a scene from the story *Paint Pots and Queens*. "The stations on the line were being painted. The engines were surprised. 'The Queen is coming,' said the painters. The engines in their shed were excited and wondered who would pull the Royal Train. 'I'm too old to pull important trains,' said Edward sadly. 'I'm in disgrace,' Gordon said gloomily. 'The Fat Controller would never choose me.' 'He'll choose me, of course,' boasted James the red engine. 'You!' Henry snorted, 'You can't climb hills. He will ask me to pull it, and I'll have a new coat of paint. You wait and see.'

"The days passed. Henry puffed about proudly, quite sure that he would be the Royal Engine. One day when it rained, his driver and fireman stretched a tarpaulin from the cab to the tender to keep themselves dry. Henry puffed into the big station. A painter was climbing a ladder above the line. Henry's smoke puffed upwards; it was thick and black. The painter choked and couldn't see. He missed his footing on the ladder, dropped his paint pot, and fell ploop on to Henry's tarpaulin. The paint poured over Henry's boiler, and trickled down each side. The paint pot perched on his dome.

"The painter clambered down and shook his brush at Henry. 'You spoil my clean paint with your dirty smoke,' he said, 'and then you take the whole lot, and make me go and fetch some more.' He stumped crossly away. The Fat Controller pushed through the crowd. 'You look like an iced cake, Henry,' he said. 'That won't do for the Royal Train. I must make other arrangements.' He walked over to the yard."

From *Gordon the Big Engine* by The Rev. W. Awdry

Poor old Henry gets covered in paint while the station is being prepared for a royal visit (above). This large and sturdy toy bag would be useful and decorative in a child's bedroom or a playroom for tidying away all sorts of toys and clutter (opposite).

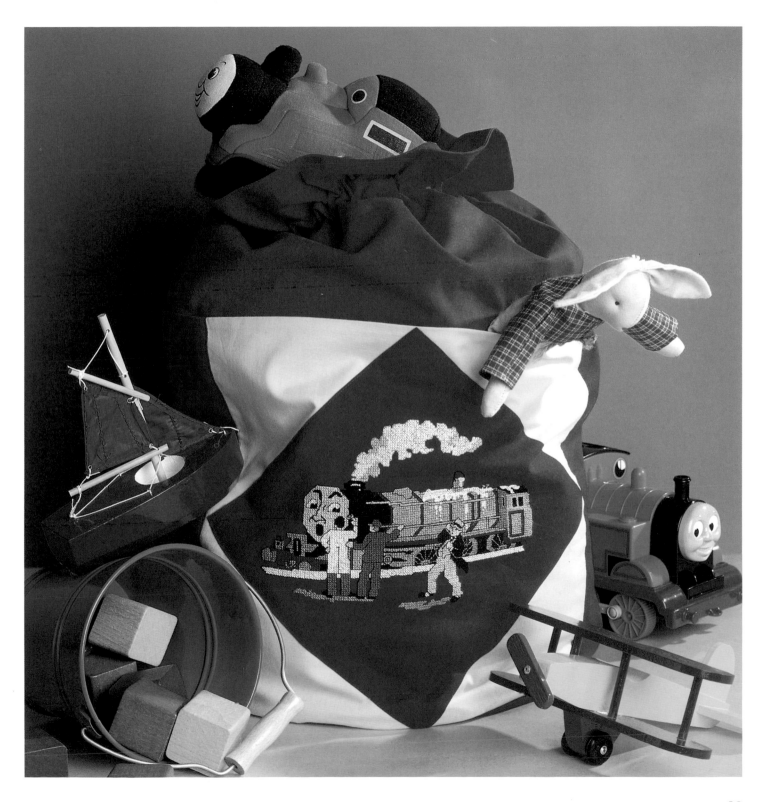

DMC	ANCHOR
700	228
704	238
725	306
310	403
Blanc	1
825	162
632	936
976	309
321	9046
451	233
453	231
754	4146

ABILITY LEVEL: *Advanced*

MEASUREMENTS

The cross stitch design measures 15 x 22cm
(6 x 8¾in)

MATERIALS

- Basic sewing kit (see page 92)
- One piece of 14-count waste canvas,
  19 x 28cm (7⅝ x 11¼in)
- A piece of interfacing, 19 x 28cm (7⅝ x 11¼in)
- Stranded cotton, one skein of each of the
  colours shown in the key (left)

- Tapestry needle, size 24-26
- A 15cm (6in) embroidery hoop
- One piece of red cotton, 112 x 200cm
  (45 x 80in)
- One piece of yellow cotton, 112 x 75cm
  (45 x 30in)
- Red and yellow thread to match
- Two wooden beads with large holes, 2.5cm
  (1in) long
- A length of sturdy blue cotton tape, 2.5 x
  150cm (1 x 60in)

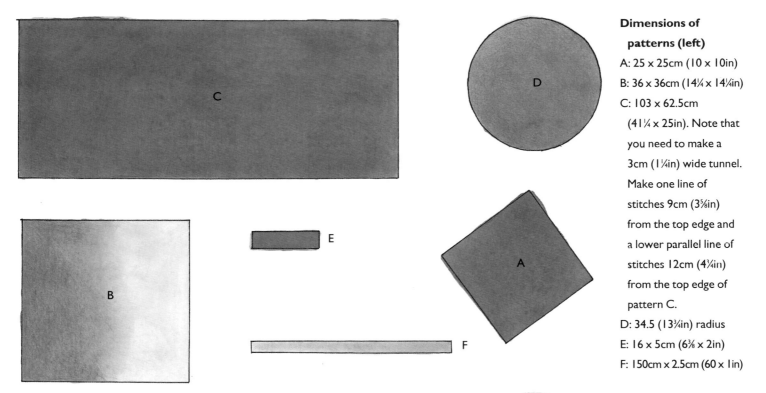

Dimensions of patterns (left)

A: 25 x 25cm (10 x 10in)

B: 36 x 36cm (14¼ x 14¼in)

C: 103 x 62.5cm (41¼ x 25in). Note that you need to make a 3cm (1¼in) wide tunnel. Make one line of stitches 9cm (3⅝in) from the top edge and a lower parallel line of stitches 12cm (4¾in) from the top edge of pattern C.

D: 34.5 (13¾in) radius

E: 16 x 5cm (6⅜ x 2in)

F: 150cm x 2.5cm (60 x 1in)

TO EMBROIDER

Use two strands separated from the skein to work the cross stitch, see page 95. Do not outline the gray shadows. Outline the wheels, the smoke from the train, the detail on the face of the train, the small windows, the yellow bar on the train and the bucket handle using two strands and working in backstitch, see page 95. Outline the pipes, the station platform line, the painter's coat, the paint and the spats using a single strand (in the appropriate colours) and for the rest of the outlines use a single strand of black, working in backstitch. Make French knots along the bar on the side of train with two strands twisting the yarn twice around the needle, see page 97. For the Fat Controller's eyes and the waistcoat buttons make French knots but with a single strand.

TO MAKE UP

1. Centre the design on the square of red cotton, see pattern A in the diagram above. Measure carefully and use basting lines as a positional guide, see page 93. Fix the hoop in the middle of the area to be stitched and start to cross stitch. Treat the finished embroidery as described on page 94.

2. First make the pockets. Cut out the square pattern B (referring to the diagram above), twice in red cotton and twice in yellow cotton. Throughout you should use a seam allowance of 1cm (⅜in). Pin, baste and machine sew a

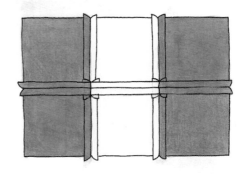

panel of yellow sandwiched between two panels of red with wrong sides together to form a rectangle. Repeat to form a second rectangle to line the pockets. Join both these rectangles along their longer edges, with wrong sides together. Press the seams after each sewing stage.

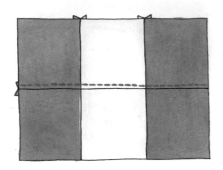

3. Turn right side up and topstitch about 0.25cm (⅛in) in from the long seam for a neat edge (see page 96).

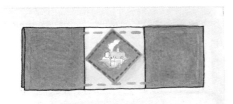

4. Fold the rectangle in half lengthways to form a double layer of fabric. Pin and baste around all four sides to hold both layers in position ready to attach to the main bag. Fold in the raw edges of the embroidered panel (pattern A). Pin and baste to the central yellow panel on the right side of the pocket to form a diamond-shaped piece of appliqué. Make sure the points of the diamond fall inside the seam allowance of the pocket.

5. Cut out pattern C (refer to the diagram on the previous page). Place this right side up on a flat surface. Pin and baste the pocket panel made in the previous steps right side up onto the lower half of the large piece of red cotton that forms the main body of the toy bag. Machine stitch the three sides of the pocket panel with large stitches. Adjust the tension and machine stitch down the dividing line of the red and yellow panels to form three separate pockets.

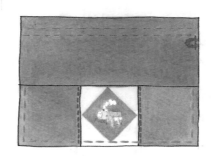

6. Cut out pattern E (refer to the diagram on the previous page) to make a loop. Fold in half lengthways, tuck in the raw edges and top stitch down the open long edge; the finished strip should be about 1.5cm (⅝in) wide. Fold in half widthways to form a loop and hand sew the ends just below the tunnelling line (marked on pattern C).

7. Take the second piece of red cotton cut out from pattern C and join it to the long edge of the main panel of the toy bag along the top edge to form a lining. Join both pieces from pattern C in

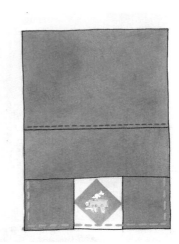

exactly the same way as you joined the pocket panel and pocket lining together (see steps 2 and 3).

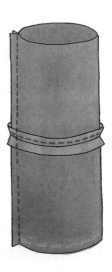

8. To form the toy bag, fold the joined main panel and lining lengthways with wrong sides facing. Pin, baste and machine sew down the open long edge to form a tube shape. Leave a gap as shown on pattern C for the tie. Press open the seam allowances.

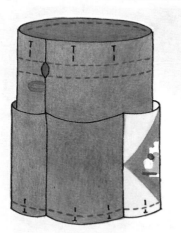

9. Turn the whole tube right side out and push the lining down inside the bag. Pin, baste and machine sew two parallel lines to form a 3cm (1¼in) wide tunnel

for the tie to pass through, as marked on pattern C. Pin the top and bottom edges of the bag aligning the centre seams so that the lining and outer layer of fabric are held in position.

10. Cut out pattern D twice. Pin, baste and machine sew the two circles wrong sides together with long stitches and leave the threads long. Pull the threads gently to ease in; this helps to fit the circular base to the bag. Mark four compass points with four pins on the base.

11. Turn the bag inside out and mark four compass points with four pins on the bottom of the bag, to align with the

four pins on the circular base made in the previous step. Ease the circular base by pulling the threads evenly at both ends to fit the circumference of the bottom of the bag. Pin, baste and machine sew the base to the bag, right sides together. To finish the raw edges either bind with bias binding (see page 97), overlock with a zigzag setting on the machine, or over-sew (see page 96). Turn the whole bag right side out.

12. Attach one end of the length of blue tape to a safety pin and push through the tunnel. Leave the ends long and tie a wooden bead on each end to secure. Fray the ends after knotting.

Materials and Techniques

Over the following pages the materials and techniques required for making your own cross stitch projects at home are fully detailed. The equipment section gives information on the types of fabrics you can use, the variety of threads available for embroidery and advice on essential pieces of equipment, from keeping a well-stocked sewing kit to more specialist items such as embroidery hoops and needles. The Techniques section explains how to centre a design on a backing fabric, how to work with special fabrics such as waste canvas and how to treat a completed piece of cross stitch so that it lasts well. There are illustrations and instructions for all sorts of useful stitches, including how to do cross stitch, work a number of different sewing stitches for making up the projects, as well as how to make your own bias binding.

Opposite With just a few inexpensive pieces of basic equipment you can get started on all kinds of cross stitch designs at home.
Below An original illustration from the story *Thomas and Bertie*, where the train engine and the bus have a cross-country race. See page **36** for a project based around this story.

Equipment

Cross stitch must be embroidered on "even-weave" fabric which has an equal number of vertical "warp" and horizontal "weft" threads per inch (2.5cm). Many of the projects in this book are worked on Aida cloth which is an even-weave fabric woven with groups of threads. Each group counts as one thread, so 14-count Aida has 14 groups per inch (2.5cm). Insert and bring up the tapestry needle through the holes in the Aida cloth so that the stitches cover the intersections of the groups of threads. Aida comes in a range of sizes, from coarse 8-count to fine 18-count. It is available in a variety of colours. Always leave a generous margin of Aida, allowing a minimum of 5cm (2in), around the outer limit of the stitched design before cutting out. In this way you will have an allowance for fixing the embroidery hoop and later for framing, mounting, attaching bias binding etc when you come to making up the project.

Before you begin to cross stitch on Aida you should neaten the raw edges either by turning them under and oversewing (see page 96) or else by folding them under and binding them with masking tape, otherwise they have a tendency to fray.

Some projects in the book require the cross stitch to be worked on waste canvas, with a backing of non-woven interfacing. Waste canvas allows you to cross stitch directly onto all sorts of fabrics (cotton, felt, denim, wool etc) which do not otherwise present a visible grid to work to. It has a contrasting thread at regular intervals to facilitate counting the rows and stitches as you are working. It ranges in mesh size from 8-count to 14-count. In this book I have only used 14-count, or 14 holes to the inch (2.5cm) waste canvas.

Non-woven interfacing is a very thin, delicate fibre which can be removed by gently tearing away after stitching through it. Used in conjunction with waste canvas it helps to provide a stable base for stitching. Position the waste canvas onto the fabric that you wish to embroider and place a layer of interfacing under the fabric. Work the cross stitch through all three layers. When the embroidery is complete, dampen the waste canvas with a cloth and it will gradually begin to soften. Gently pull away the horizontal threads with a pair of tweezers and then the vertical threads, one by one. Carefully tear away the layer of interfacing. To treat the finished cross stitch, see page 94.

Embroidery hoops come in a range of sizes; the size most commonly used in this book is a 15cm (6in) diameter hoop. Use the wooden-framed hoop to keep the backing fabric taut while you cross stitch and it will help you sew neat stitches and give a good overall finish.

EMBROIDERY HOOPS

Although you can cross stitch while holding fabric in the hand, it is far more satisfactory to use a hoop. The hoop consists of two wooden rings, the larger with an adjustable butterfly screw. To fix the fabric onto the hoop, position the fabric over the smaller ring and fix the larger ring around it, tightening the screw so that the fabric is held really taut. Working on a hoop retains the shape and tension of the fabric and so helps you to work the stitches evenly; it also enables you to see how the design is progressing. If you need to reposition the hoop over an area of embroidered fabric (for instance if the design exceeds the size of your hoop) protect the cross stitch that comes into contact with the hoop with tissue paper. Hoops are available in various diameters.

NEEDLES

Work cross stitch using a tapestry needle. This has a large eye for easy threading and a blunt end so that it does not pierce and separate the fabric threads.

91

You can also use a tapestry needle for basting. A size 24-26 tapestry needle is suitable for all the projects featured in the book, except for the pencil case project which requires a larger size 20 needle.

THREADS

Various kinds of threads are suitable for cross stitch. In all but one project in the book I have specified DMC stranded cottons and given the equivalent colour codes for Anchor yarns. Note that stranded cotton consists of several (usually six) fine threads that are loosely twisted together in a skein. Cut off a suitable length of

thread from the skein and separate the number of threads required, as indicated in the instructions for each project. On 14-count Aida you would normally use two strands for the basic design; on finer 16-count Aida a single strand of thread is best. By varying the number of threads that you use you can vary the texture of the finished cross stitch, highlight some areas and also create very fine lines of stitching. In the pencil case project on page 46 I used a single strand from a pure wool skein on 14-count Aida. By separating off individual strands it is also possible to cross stitch in wool. The specified threads are colourfast.

BASIC SEWING KIT

Many of the projects require additional sewing once you have completed the cross stitch design. Your sewing kit should be equipped with the following:

- Large scissors for cutting out patterns
- Small scissors for cutting threads
- Tape measure
- Variety of coloured threads
- Variety of sewing needles
- Basic sewing machine
- Quick unpick

- Thimble
- Plenty of pins
- Several safety pins
- Tweezers
- Tracing paper for patterns
- Fabric marker

How to cross stitch

HOW TO CENTRE A CROSS STITCH DESIGN

As a starting point, refer to the coloured cross stitch chart that accompanies each project and check the dimensions of each design given alongside. Find the centre point of the design with the aid of the arrows that are marked on two sides of the chart. From the vertical arrow, trace a straight line downwards through the chart; from the horizontal arrow trace another straight line across through the chart. Where they intersect marks the centre of the design.

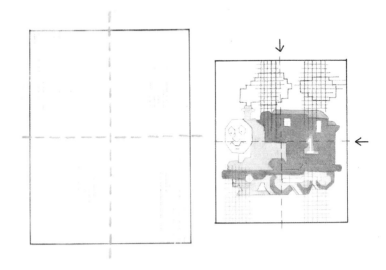

To centre the design on a piece of Aida cloth, find the middle of the fabric by folding it in half once, and once again so that it is folded exactly into quarters. Press the folds gently with a cool iron. Then open up the Aida again and where the two fold lines meet, mark the mid-point of the Aida with a fabric pen. Baste along the pressed fold lines in contrasting thread to give a positional guide. Align the centre of the design on the chart with the mid-point on the Aida cloth, which is where the two basting lines intersect.

If you are working on waste canvas you cannot fold the canvas because it is stiff and starched. Instead, refer to the measurements given in each project for the

dimensions of the finished design, use these as a guide. Your stitching area must be greater than these dimensions, and you must allow a margin for fixing the hoop. Establish a boundary for the design, divide the designated area into equal quarters by marking a vertical and a horizontal line, either with a fabric marker or with basting stitches in contrasting thread; they cross at the mid-point of the canvas. Repeat to mark the mid-point on the piece of interfacing. Use the basting lines as a guide to line up all three mid-points of the waste canvas, the interfacing and the chart. Secure all three layers together with firm basting.

TO WORK THE CROSS STITCH

Each project is accompanied by at least one chart and each square on the chart represents one cross stitch. The coloured squares in the chart correspond to the relevant key and the numbers in the key indicate the colour codes for the yarns. Where there are blank squares in the chart leave the fabric plain. The arrows on two sides of the chart will help you find the mid-point of the design. Keep a careful count of the stitches as you work and follow the whole design accurately. Once you have fixed the fabric centrally inside the embroidery hoop, start stitching in the middle of the design and work outwards. Some cross stitchers like to work all the stitches of one colour before starting on the others. However, this can lead to mistakes, especially when you have a large area to cover. It is better, therefore, to work each small area of one colour and then change the thread to work the adjacent stitches in the next colour. For example, you might want to work the front of an engine in black, then change colour to stitch the engine's side. Building up the design in this way will help you to make sure that the finished piece is accurately worked. You may like to use a ruler or a piece of cardboard to mark off each area of the chart as you complete it, this will help you concentrate on one area at a time.

TREATING THE FINISHED DESIGN

When you have completed a design, and removed all the waste canvas and interfacing if used (see page 90), you should wash the finished item in warm water with a gentle soap powder. While you are working the embroidery, the fabric may become grubby from contact with your hands, so it will benefit from a gentle wash. To dry the cross stitch, roll it up in a towel. When it is still a little damp, place the embroidery face down on a towel and press with an iron on a low setting on the wrong side of the fabric to flatten the finished design. Allow the canvas to dry thoroughly before you make it up into a finished item.

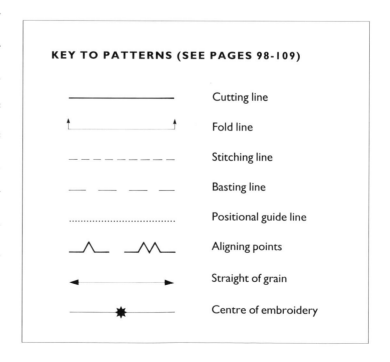

KEY TO PATTERNS (SEE PAGES 98-109)

————————	Cutting line
	Fold line
– – – – – – –	Stitching line
— — — —	Basting line
....	Positional guide line
⋀_ ⋀⋀_	Aligning points
◄——————►	Straight of grain
—✸—	Centre of embroidery

The stitches

CROSS STITCH

You can work cross stitch in horizontal, vertical or diagonal rows. To fill an area it is best to work in horizontal rows. First work a number of diagonal stitches from right to left, then work back over the diagonal threads from left to right so that each stitch forms a cross (see below). If you work in diagonal rows complete each stitch before you begin the next one.

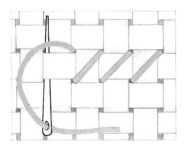 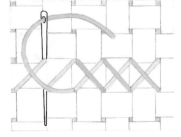

STARTING AND FINISHING

To start or finish a thread do not tie a knot as it can show up as an unsightly bump on the finished embroidery and it may eventually come undone 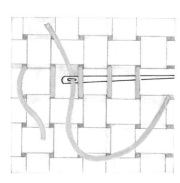 and loosen stitches in the design. Instead, begin by inserting the needle and leave a tail of thread which you can then catch and hold fast in the back of the first completed stitches on the wrong side of the fabric. To finish, run the needle and thread through the backs of already worked stitches and break off.

HALF CROSS STITCH

Literally half a cross stitch, so that you work a single diagonal stitch to complement full cross stitches. This stitch is similar to tent stitch, but uses less thread 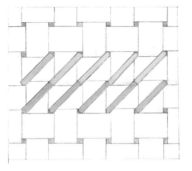 and is more suitable when producing small-scale designs such as those in this book.

BACKSTITCH

Bring the needle up to the right side of the fabric, insert it about 3mm (⅛in) to one side (preferably to the right) of the emerging thread. Work a longer 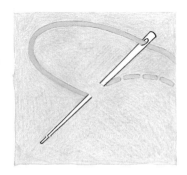 stitch on the wrong side so that the needle emerges 3mm (⅛in) to the left of the previous stitch.

BASTING

Loose running stitches that are longer on the right side of the fabric and shorter on the reverse side. Use a contrasting thread for a guideline, either to centre a design or to mark the path of a seam. To ease fabric into a gather, pull the ends of basting stitches with equal pressure. Remove basting stitches after sewing.

TAILOR'S TACKS

A useful way to make a removable marker on a pattern. Use a contrasting thread to make several loops and knot them very loosely. Sew through the pattern paper and the fabric to make helpful marks for lining up pattern pieces when making up some of the projects. Snip to undo when all the sewing is completed.

TOPSTITCH

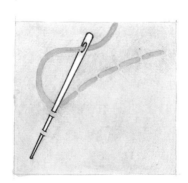

A neat line of small stitches, butting up end to end so almost no space divides them on either side of the fabric. Work by machine or by hand on the right side of the fabric to provide a strong, visible seam. Work long stitch by the same method, increasing the length of the stitch on the right side of the fabric.

OVERSEWING

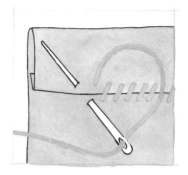

A series of diagonal stitches sloping from left to right on the wrong side of the fabric, and small catching stitches in the main fabric that barely show on the right side. Use as a form of hemming; turn under the raw edges, fold along the seam allowance and oversew to prevent fraying.

SLIPSTITCH

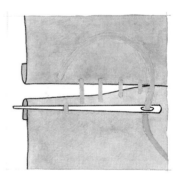

Use to join two folded edges together. Work on the right side of the fabric, with the folded edges butting together. Insert the needle so the thread runs about 0.5cm (¼in) just inside the top of one fold, bring the needle out and insert it into the opposite fold with a small catching stitch. Pull the folds together and repeat. Do not pucker the fabric.

CHAIN STITCH

A useful stitch for making a curve. Bring the needle and thread up in one hole of Aida or waste canvas on the right side, form a loop and 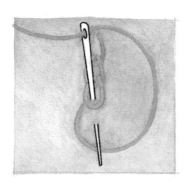 re-insert the needle into the same hole, so that the loop remains. Then pass the needle under two threads of canvas on the reverse side, keeping a vertical line. Next bring up the needle to the right side again so that it emerges two holes below the first hole, pass the thread over the loop just made so that it is held close against the canvas. Always re-insert the needle into the hole it emerged from in the last loop.

FRENCH KNOT

A round, slightly raised stitch like a bobble, useful for representing eyes, buttons etc. Bring the thread through to the right side 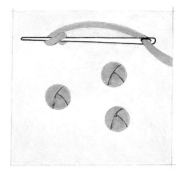 of the canvas, position the needle horizontally, pointing left. Wrap the thread around the needle once or twice as desired, and then turn the needle so that it points upwards. Insert the needle into the canvas one hole above and to the right of the first hole.

BLANKET STITCH

Work over a raw or folded edge to secure and to dec- 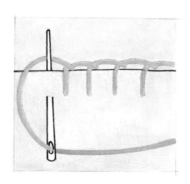 orate; use a contrasting thread for emphasis. On the right side of the fabric, insert the needle the required distance at right angles to the edge. Make small neat or more exaggerated blanket stitches according to the effect you desire. Bring the needle up just on the edge of the right side of the fabric, loop the thread behind the needle and pull through to form a loop. Continue to form a series of decorative loops.

BIAS BINDING

Essentially a long, narrow strip of fabric. It can be purchased ready-made with pre-folded edges. However, it is simple  to make. The bias lies diagonally across the weave of a fabric. To find the true bias of a piece of fabric, fold a straight raw edge so that it lies parallel to the selvedge and forms a triangle – the base of the triangle is the bias line. Mark and cut out strips of fabric parallel to this line, according to the width you require.

97

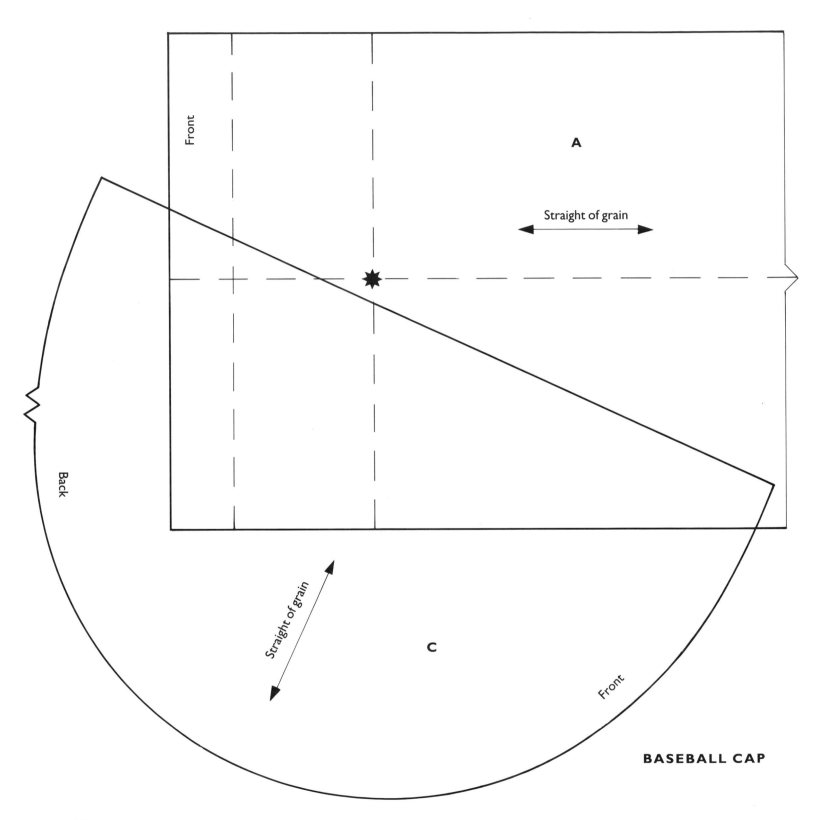

Front

A

Straight of grain

Back

Straight of grain

C

Front

BASEBALL CAP

98

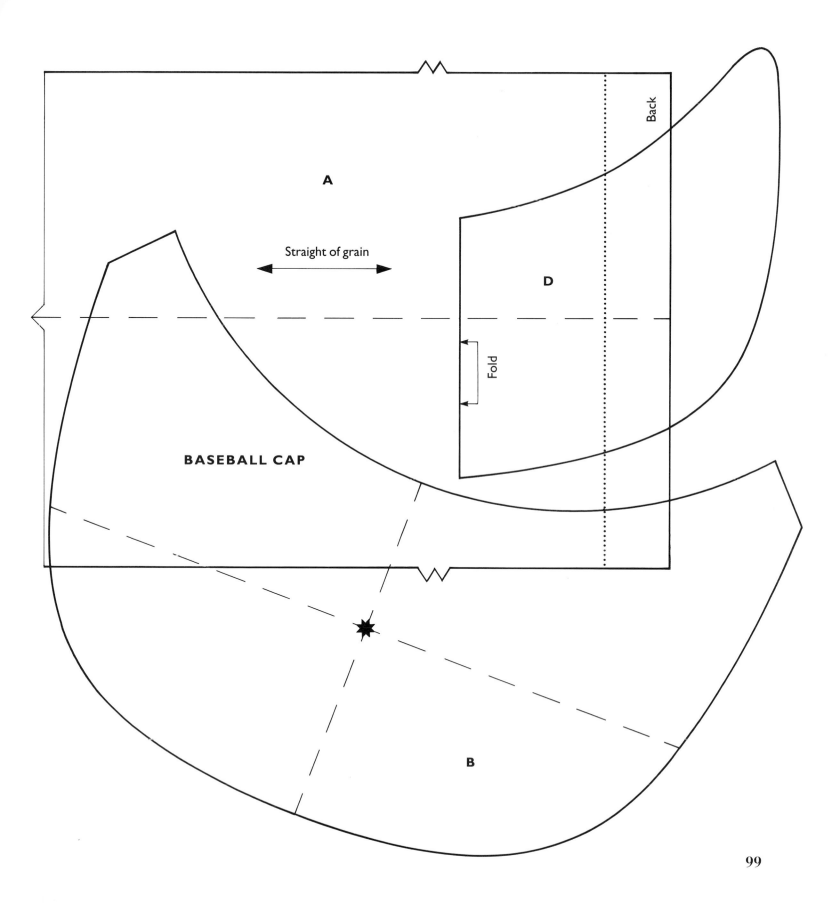

A

Straight of grain

D

Back

Fold

BASEBALL CAP

B

SLIPPERS

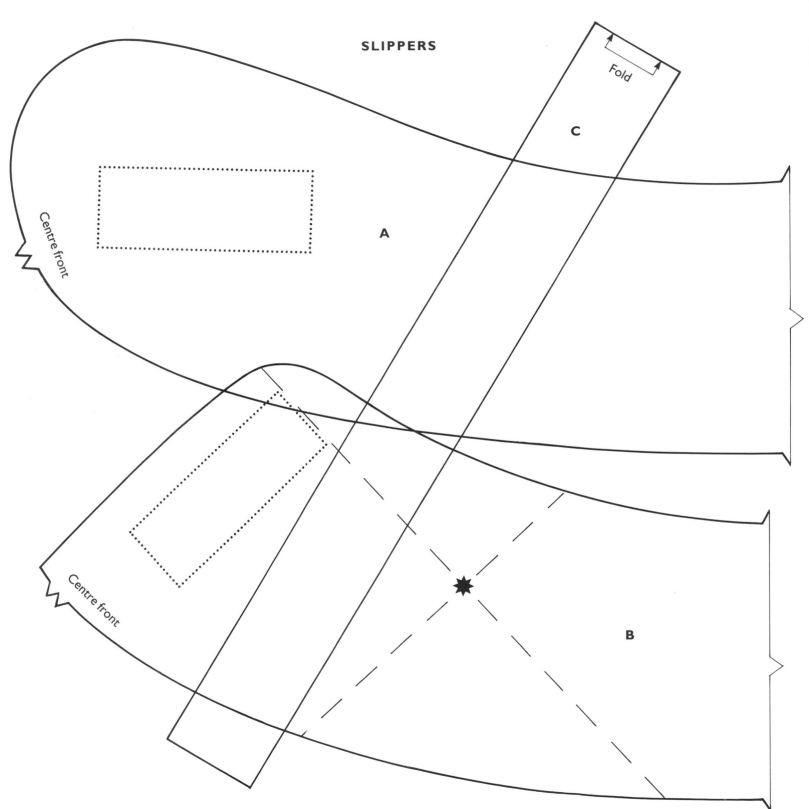

Fold

C

A

Centre front

Centre front

B

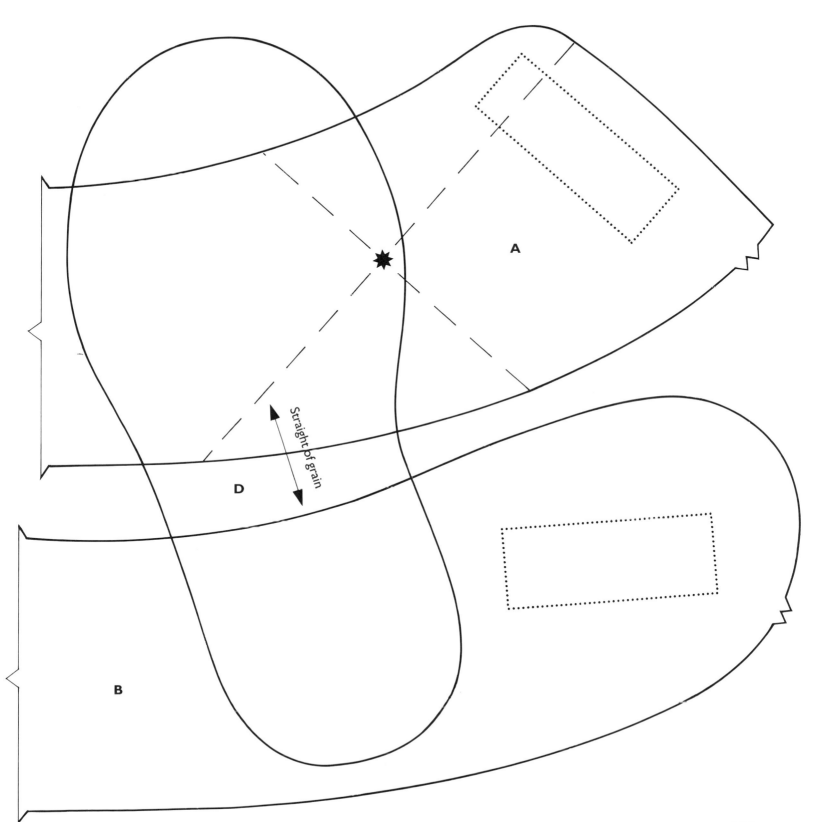

Straight of grain

A

B

D

101

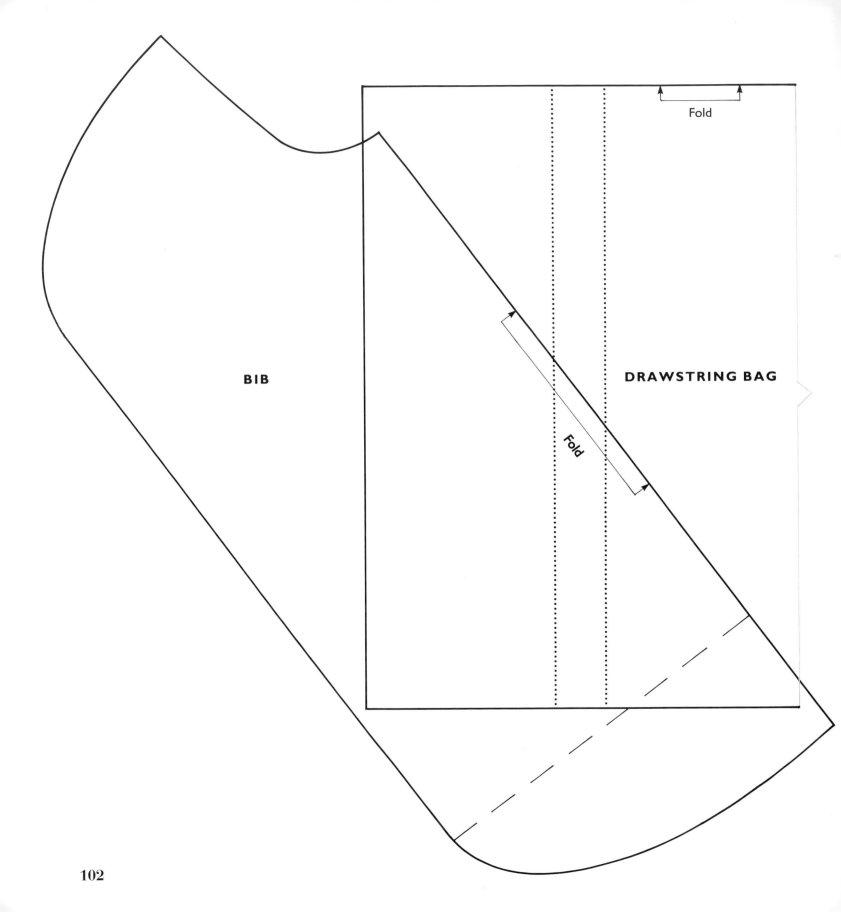

BIB

DRAWSTRING BAG

Fold

Fold

Fold

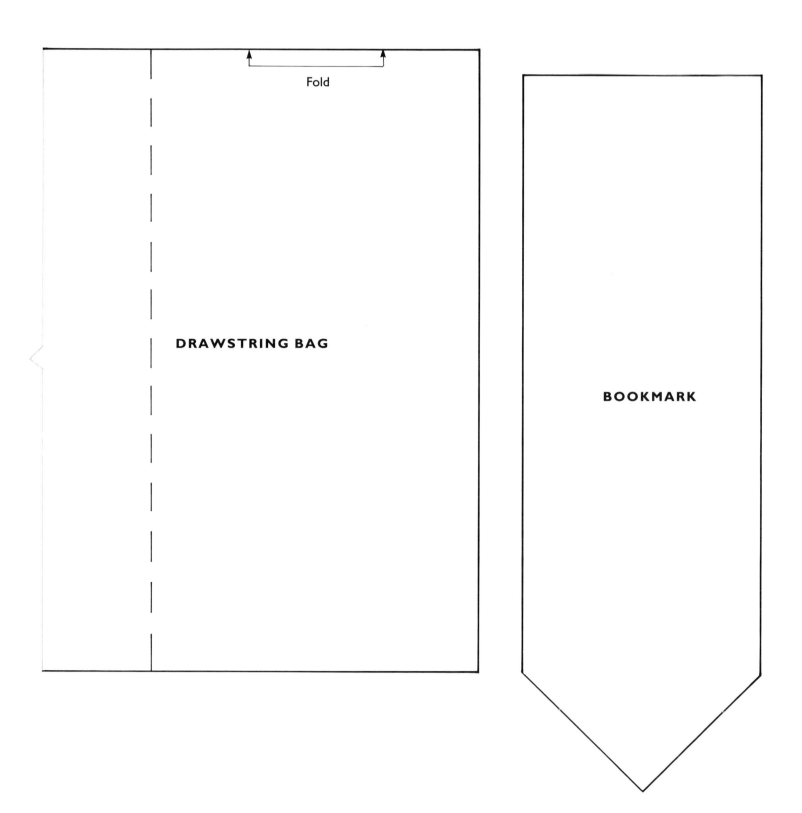

Fold

DRAWSTRING BAG

BOOKMARK

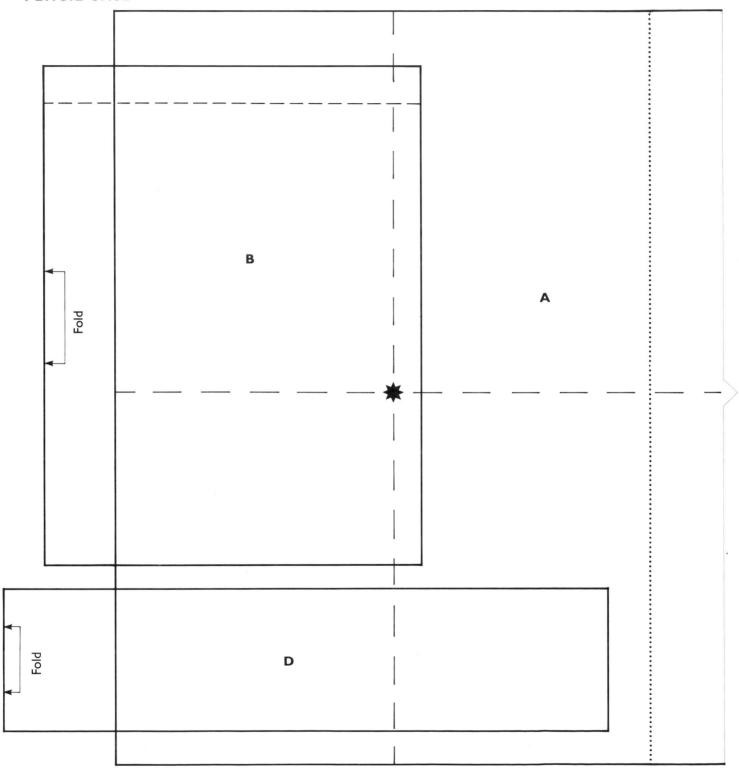

A

B

Fold

D

Fold

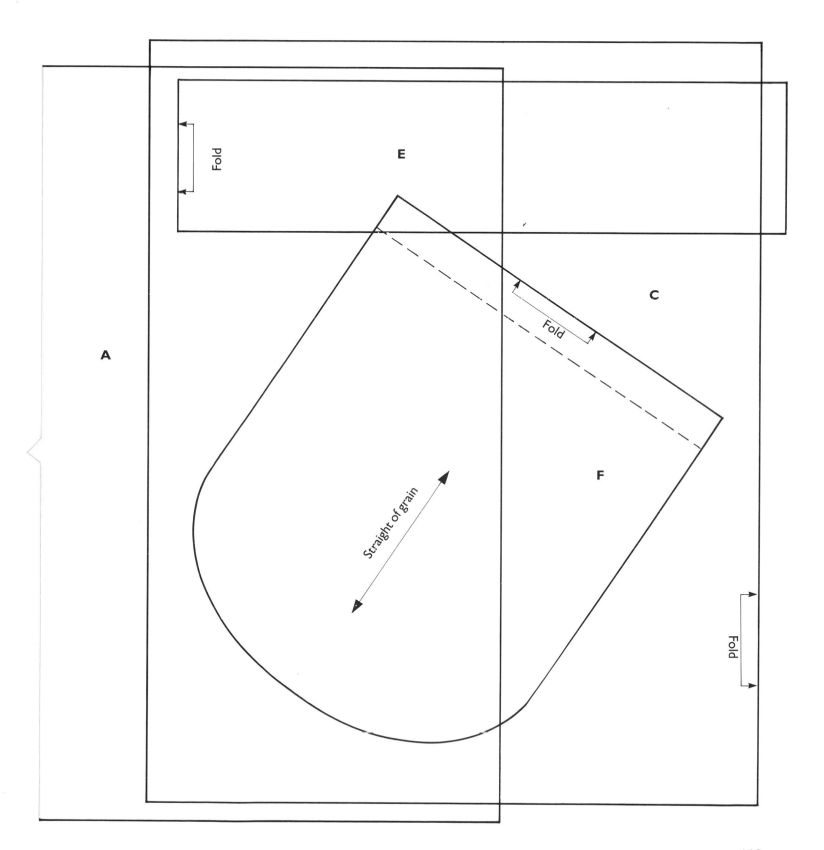

A

E

C

F

Fold

Fold

Fold

Straight of grain

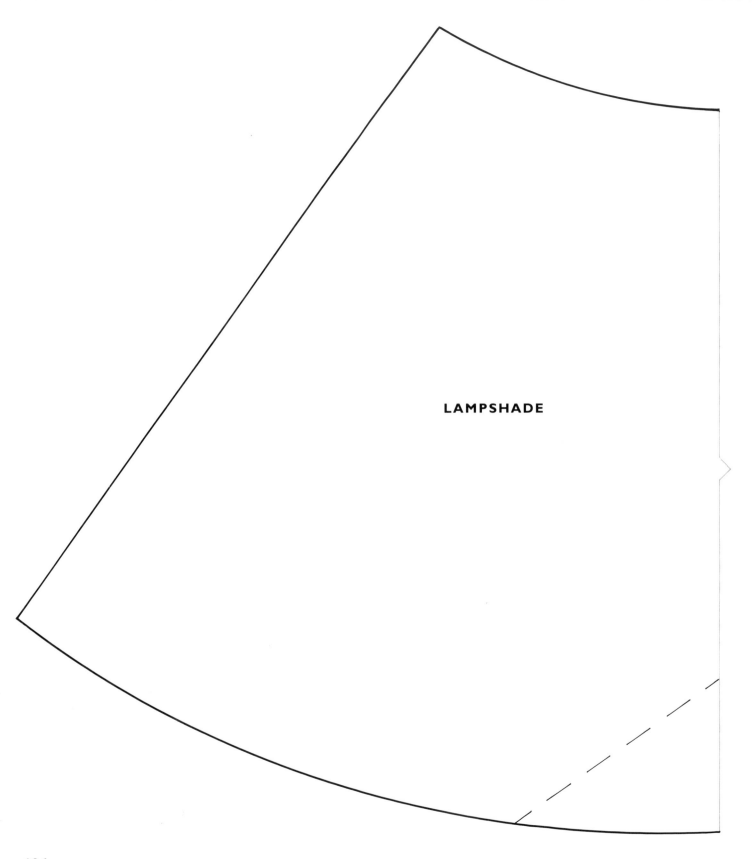

LAMPSHADE

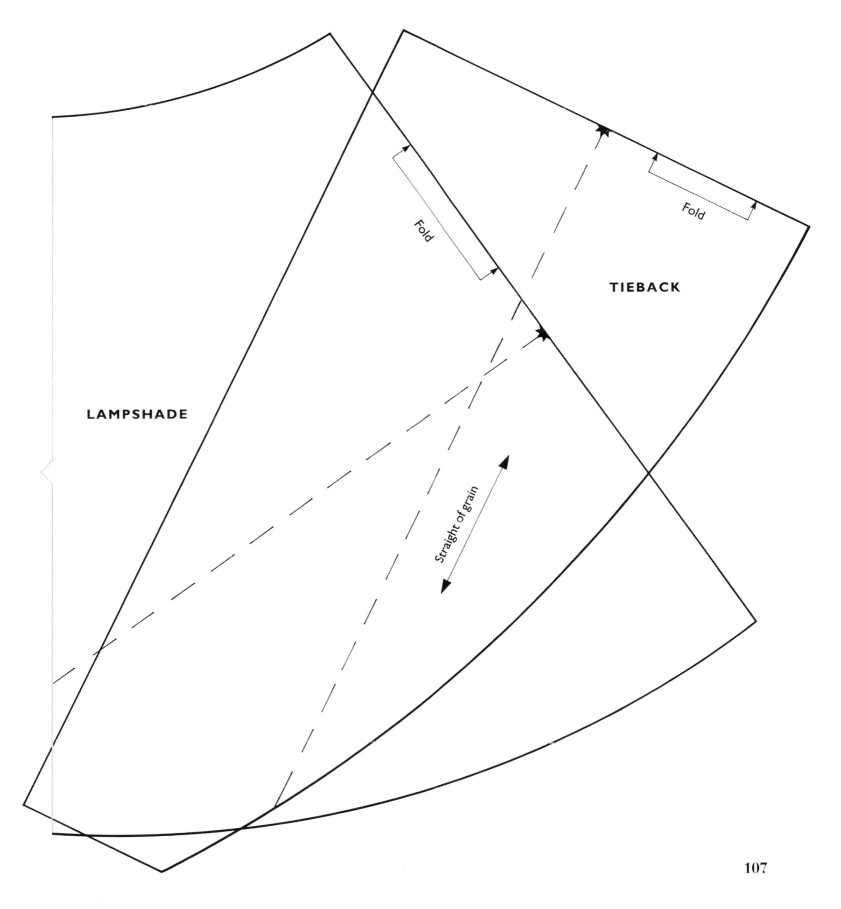

LAMPSHADE

TIEBACK

Fold

Fold

Straight of grain

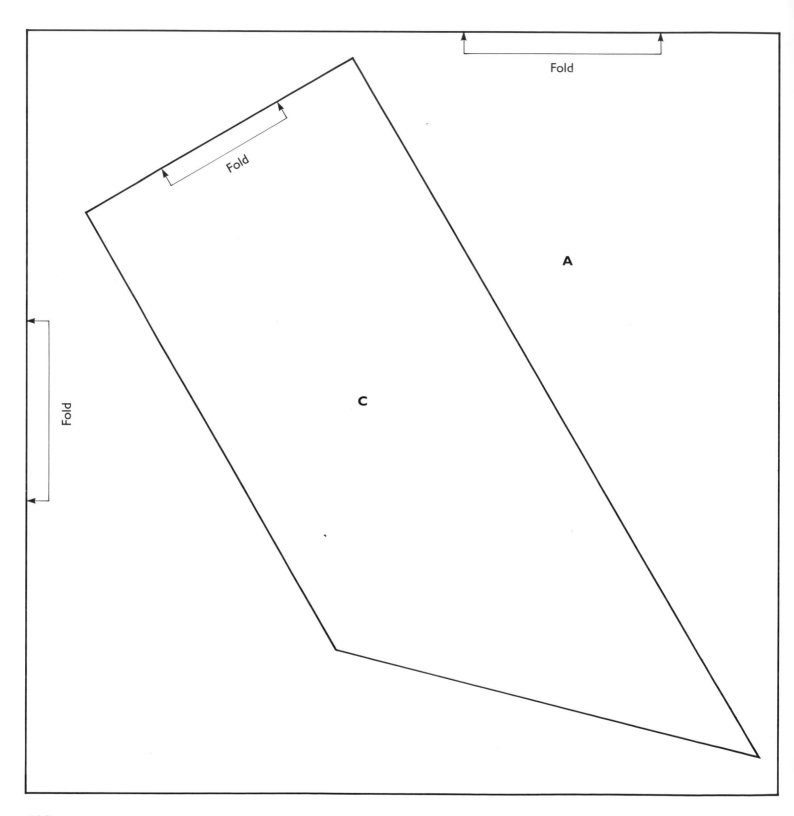

Fold

Fold

Fold

A

C

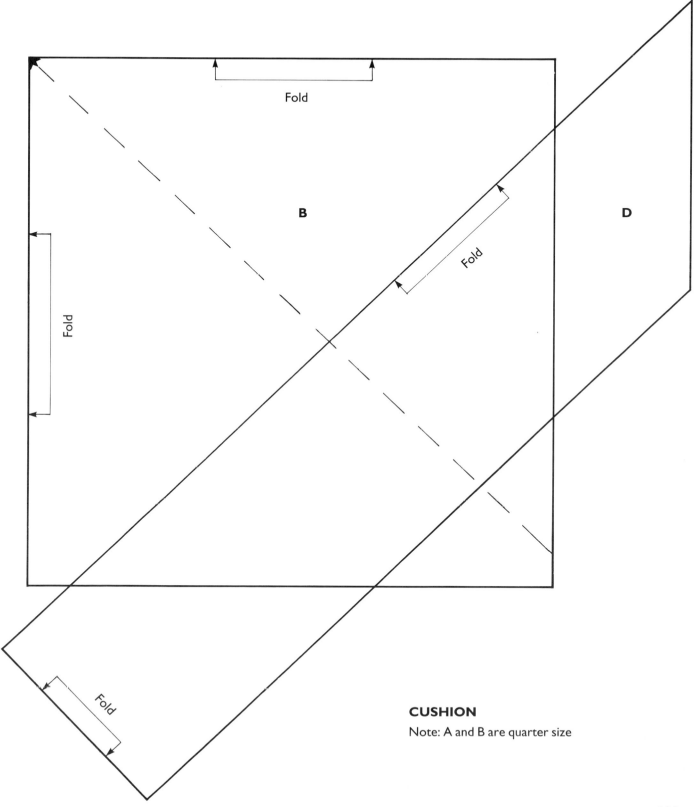

CUSHION

Note: A and B are quarter size

Suppliers

NEEDLEWORK PRODUCTS

All DMC, Anchor and Paterna yarns used in this book are available from the relevant stockists listed below and many other needlecraft outlets the world over. The addresses given below are the head offices – contact them for advise on local availability of yarns. Good haberdasheries also supply other products, including embroidery hoops, cards, needles, scissors etc.

UK:

DMC Creative World
Pullman Road
Wigston
Leicester
Leicestershire LE18 2DY

Coats Patons Crafts
McMullen Road
Darlington
Co Durham DL1 1YQ
(Anchor yarns)

The Craft Collection Ltd
Terry Mills
Westfield Road
Horbury
Wakefield
West Yorkshire WR4 6HD
(Paterna yarns. Also distribute throughout Europe)

USA:

The DMC Corporation
Port Kearny
Building 10
South Kearny
New Jersey 07032

Coats and Clark
Greenville
South Carolina
(Anchor yarns)

Australia and New Zealand:

DMC
51-66 Carrington Road
Marrickville
New South Wales 2204

Warnaar Trading Co Ltd
376 Ferry Road
PO Box 19567
Christchurch
(DMC yarns)

Coats Patons Crafts
Mulgrave 3170
Australia
(Anchor yarns)

Altamira
34 Murphy Street
South Yarra
Melbourne 3141
Australia
(Paterna yarns)

The Stitching Co Ltd
PO Box 74/269
Market Road
Auckland
New Zealand
(Paterna yarns)

Europe:

Dollfuss Mieg & Co
10 avenue Ledru-Rollin
75579 Paris
France
(DMC yarns)

BTW
Stader landstr. 41-43
D-2820 Bremen 77
Germany
(DMC yarns)

DMC
Ciale Italia 84
1-20020 Lainate
Milano
Italy

DMC
7/9 rue du Pavillon
B-1210 Brussels
Belgium

Coats Sartel Loisirs
59392 Wattrelos Cedex
France
(Anchor yarns)

Coats Mez GmbH
79337 Kensingen
Germany
(Anchor yarns)

Cucirini Cantoni Coats
20124 Milano
Italy
(Anchor yarns)

Index

ACKNOWLEDGMENTS

Thank you to Wendy Cockburn for helping me to embroider the projects for this book with great care and patience. Also thank you to my husband, Raymond Turvey, for the organization of the embroidery charts.